Contents

ELIZA HOPE-BROWN

Sanctuary

every new beginning comes from some other beginning's end...

Second edition

ISBN: 9798386540890

Editing by Daisy Hollands

This book was professionally typeset on Reedsy.
Find out more at reedsy.com

Sweet Inevitability

Two souls intertwined across time
Always destined to find each other
No matter what it takes
Or the consequences

Even in their darkest moments
They're fated to find each other
Like pieces of a beautiful cosmic puz-
zle
That always find a way to click into
place

One of them always knowing
Understanding the sweet inevitabil-
ity
Particles of the stars once blown
apart
Always finding their way home

~ EHB

Acknowledgement

Writing acknowledgements isn't something you set out to write when you begin to write a book. When I first started this, I didn't even know what I was writing would go on to become a book. But throughout, I've had support and love from a very dear friend who has acted as my confidante and been my editor for the whole process. Without Daisy glittering my words and crying when I wrote something she liked, this book you hold would simply not exist.

Thank you, Daisy.

I want to thank my parents too, who have always supported and encouraged me in all my creative endeavours and efforts. They're the rock I consistently keep coming back to, whether tides are low or high.

A big thanks also has to go to my cat, Morley, who did his best to keep me distracted when I needed it, mainly when he wanted fussing or feeding.

The Playlist

I have always been a lover of music from a very young age. As cliched as it sounds, music is regularly the soundtrack to my life and you'll often find me plugged into something listening to my favourite songs.

Large portions of this story you're about to read were written to specific songs that I listened to on repeat.

I have collected them into a single Spotify playlist for you to listen to and enjoy while you read.

Enjoy!

Chapter 1

"Something in your eyes, makes me want to lose myself "

Slipping in a blank memory card, the photographer placed his hand easily through the wrist strap of his Sony A9 Mirrorless camera and called over the next athlete. As she walked across the studio, he could feel her nerves as if they were his own. Taking her position over the little piece of pink gaffer tape, stuck in an X on the floor in front of her, she looked up, wishing this could all be over already.

"Okay, just turn a little to your left, and hold the ball just slightly higher on your hip for me, please?" He spoke gently. She was shaking a little, unable to fight the feeling of being exposed.

"Lift your chin for me?" He continued, smiling to reassure her, "perfect."

She tried to do as she was asked but the sticky feeling of being self-conscious clung to her skin like a sickness. She didn't feel anything close to perfect. She had the impression that he was detached from what was happening, just going through the motions and that he didn't particularly care who was in front of his camera lens at all. He must have done this hundreds of times before.

The words of the text message from her fiancé rang in her head. "Just hurry up and come home. I have stuff to do." She'd upset him again, but how, she didn't know.

The photographer pressed the shutter for the last time before needing to adjust the set in front of him, and realised as the last image flashed up in his eye piece, that something had changed. The blonde girl in front of him had lost focus for a second and her eyes had drifted away from him slightly. She looked lost in thought and adrift, but at the same time, breathtakingly beautiful. The image knocked him out of his well-rehearsed stride; bringing the camera down from in front of his face, he composed himself quickly.

"That's great, thanks. Go relax for a bit. We need to change some bits up here."

~

"You did great, you know?" He remarked, moving next to where she stood near a table full of refreshments during the break.

"Thank you," she replied quietly, giving him space to pour himself a coffee. "It doesn't feel like something I'm good at."

"That's normal though for someone who doesn't do this all the time. But you're doing really well." He'd done this bit previously, numerous times; trying to put a nervous model at ease so he could get better shots later on in the day. But this time, he was also using it as an excuse to talk to this girl, not fully knowing why. The last image shot of her remained in his mind's eye as they stood next to each other.

"Is this what you do most of the time?" She asked, wanting to shift focus away from herself and onto him, although the guilt of talking to another man made her feel ashamed. She thought back to the text message.

"Yeah, a little. Some event stuff. Some documentary photography. Just depends really. What I do is quite specific really but I have different ways of doing it," he replied. He never quite knew how to describe what he did for a living.

"Sounds good," the girl replied. She felt awkward but he seemed nice and was clearly just trying to help her feel relaxed. She felt guilty for feeling guilty.

"Don't worry," he said, noticing her apprehension, "the next set up is much easier. You just get to throw the ball around. Which I guess you're ok with?"

That made her laugh. A sound that didn't escape her all that often. "Yeah, I think even I can manage that, smart guy!"

~

Hitting import on his MacBook a few minutes later, he surveyed the room. He noticed the gorgeous blonde woman was with a taller dark haired lady, who he'd photographed earlier. They seemed to be friends. But the moment that they were sharing appeared to be more tense and distressed than friendly. He was pulled away from his observation by the need to help move a light stand.

~

Two hours later, with his assistant starting to break down the set, he shook hands with the brand manager and said his goodbyes to the players he'd worked with during the day. He noticed the blonde girl kept herself at the back of the group, anxiously typing on her phone. As she looked up, she realised the rest of the group had already drifted away and she was left standing with him.

"Thanks for today." she said awkwardly, desperate to leave.

"I should be thanking you. I hope you like the images when the campaign comes out," he replied, stepping back to let her pass and leave.

"Yeah. Anyway, see ya." She hurried away.

Curiously he watched her half-running towards her car. Her dark haired friend followed behind and the photographer overheard her calling "Laura, wait! What's wrong?"

Her reply had a panicked tone to it. "I need to go. I'm sorry. I have to get home."

THE GIRL SHE WAS

She doesn't feel like herself. Not anymore. She was different once.

Now she is like a watered down version, pale and thin. She slips through the cracks, unnoticed. She fades into the background, afraid of saying the wrong thing. She grows sharp edges and won't let anyone get close to her.

CHAPTER 1

She doesn't know how she came to be like this, how she ended up here. She only remembers the way she used to be – wild and reckless. Bold and unapologetic.

~LANG LEAV

Chapter 2

"She got me wishing that she could stay."

Two years later, Dan Muir stood in a line waiting for coffee in a half empty Terminal 5 in Heathrow Airport. It was 4am and he was bone weary. It was always the same when he travelled. Regardless of the time of day of his flight, Dan never felt particularly well-rested as adrenaline and excitement usually kept him on the edge for a few days leading up to a departure.

This trip would be no different. Hired by an up-and -coming sportswear brand, his job was to shoot a campaign for their yoga clothing range across multiple locations in Istanbul. He'd spent the week prior, planning his side of the trip and liaising with the firm's media team, making sure everything was in order and that nothing had been missed.

At 38, he'd been a photographer all his life in some way, shape or form. Following his passion for creativity out of school, he'd found himself working as a junior photographer for a local paper; eventually working his way up to being a sought-after commercial photographer. Over the years, he'd tried many different styles in the genre but the last decade had seen him falling in love with a documentary style of photography and now he spent his days being paid handsomely to travel the world shooting campaigns and events.

His career had made him a frequent traveller. And while this commercial studio shoot wasn't all that exciting compared to some, it was a few days' work in Istanbul and a payout of £10,000 which he didn't really feel he could turn down. "I make money to make art. So I don't have to make art to make money," Dan had told his assistant James, when the younger apprentice had raised his perfectly sculpted eyebrow in question of the booking on the calendar. "Plus you're coming too!" He added with a wink.

~

"Who's next please?" The unenthusiastic barista droned. The customer in front of him shuffled off with his extra tall, double cream, double sugar latte and chocolate cookie in hand, leaving Dan at the front of the queue.

Moving forward, he muttered "Regular black coffee please," making minimal eye contact. It was too early for these kinds of base social interactions. He just wanted a coffee and if this crappy offering was it, then so be it. The caffeine would hit his veins and he could try and get something tastier later. He watched as the girl behind the counter filled a dirty portafilter with ground coffee and slammed it into a grubby espresso machine on the bar at the back of the small coffee hut. He inwardly rolled his eyes at the prospect of an awful drink.

"I thought you'd be more of a flat white guy."

The sweet female voice behind him caught him off guard, but he recognised it instantly. In his morning weariness, Dan hadn't realised someone familiar had been standing next in line. But there she stood. Laura Gray was 5'3" tall and softly beautiful in a way that left one breathless. Her blonde hair, which had been in tight plaits the last time he saw her, sat loosely on her shoulders. Those bright blue eyes, however, were unforgettable. They had a mysterious way of sparkling when she smiled and her gentle laugh, when she let it come out to play, was infectious. They'd first met on location for a sports brand shoot two years previously where they had chatted casually about his work while waiting for lights and gear to be repositioned.

Dan remembered how he'd felt somewhat drawn to the woman, although he couldn't put his finger on why at the time. Sure she was attractive, but there was something else. The photographer had found himself questioning it regularly over the time since their last meeting, especially if he saw her on TV or she came up in conversation in rugby circles. Rugby was both her profession and her passion.

Standing here now, she made him nervous and excited at the same time. Dan smiled awkwardly. It was 4am, but Laura had a way of making him feel awkward without even trying, irrespective of the time.

"I'm far too much of a coffee snob these days to drink milky coffee." The joke wasn't as funny as it sounded in his head and he groaned inwardly but she smiled anyway. She was that kind of person.

"Please tell me you're not having some ridiculously named coffee this early in the morning?" He smiled a half smile, trying to act cool.

"Regular skinny latte please," Laura asked of the young girl behind the counter, who grimaced. She hated customers flirting with each other while she made coffee, it was far too early to listen to some old guy crash and burn so tragically.

Dan felt guilty for his stupid question. He'd never been very good at this kind of stuff, more comfortable hidden behind a camera or a computer screen. His heart was pounding and he felt his palms getting annoyingly sweaty.

"Sorry. I'm not very good first thing in the morning. It takes me a little while and a certain amount of caffeine, to speak coherently and not sound like an arsehole."

He just wanted the ground to swallow him up and he would have understood if she'd just taken her coffee and walked away, never to look back.

God, she was as beautiful as he remembered her being. It made him nervous. Instead he just tried to focus on the barista who was making a real hash of his Americano; arguably one of the easiest possible coffees to make.

Laura just smiled. "Don't worry, I'm not much of a people person myself. I'm off on a girls' weekend for my friend's

30th birthday. Hopefully seeing a different city will shake the cobwebs out if you know what I mean?"

He did. Dan knew that she had been through a rough break-up a few months beforehand, a friend of a friend had mentioned it in passing. Hearing what she'd been through made him hurt on her behalf. No one should have to go through that, and especially not someone as lovely as Laura.

~

The pair paid for their overpriced coffees and said their goodbyes. As they made to leave, they realised they were both walking in the same direction through the airport.

"Where are you heading to?" He asked curiously.

Checking her boarding pass, tucked in her pink covered passport, Laura replied "Erm, Gate 9, the 6:05 to Rome. Never been to Italy! You?"

Dan felt his eyebrows furrow as he tried to make sense of what she'd just said, then unlocked his phone to show her his digital boarding pass.

"Gate 9. 6:05 to Rome and then connecting to Istanbul, my assistant and I have a shoot out there. He flew out yesterday to set up ahead of me."

"Ha! No way?" She said, as taken aback as the photographer was.

CHAPTER 2

~

Rather than finding an empty seat to wait for her friends at the nearby gate, Laura sat down next to Dan carrying on their conversation, looking out over the planes and boarding gates, which filled the dark sky with an array of colours and flashing lights. She explained that the rest of the girls had stayed in Duty-Free but for her, it was too early for that, so she'd told them to meet her at the gate afterwards.

Even though it was June, the terminal felt cool at this early hour and they both cradled their coffees in a vain attempt to leech the warmth from the beige paper cups.

Laura noticed the photographer's large roller case beside him. Bigger than her carry-on bag, it was about as big as would be allowed on either of his flights today, she imagined. She spotted at least two luggage tags from previous trips attached to the handles so she guessed it hadn't been purchased just for this trip, although it looked pristine. He clearly took care of his things.

"So as a coffee snob, do you bring your own coffee machine on trips?" Laura quipped, motioning to the black case next to Dan.

He paused for breath. *Don't try to be clever. Don't try to be clever!*

"No, it's my camera case. I keep it with me at all times when I fly. I can always buy clothes and stuff when I reach a destination if I lose my luggage, but it's a bit harder to replace this stuff," he tapped the bag next to his leg, "so it stays with me." Laura nodded. That made sense.

"And anyway, the coffee machine is too big to take on the flight, so it was shipped separately two days ago…" He smirked and hoped to God that she didn't think he was a knobhead.

The joke landed and the pretty blonde chuckled. "I thought so. To be honest, I was a bit disappointed when you said it was *only* cameras." Their eyes met as they laughed. "What are you going to do on the flights though? You have no other stuff to keep you entertained!"

Dan undid the uppermost zip of the black Think Tank Airport International V3 flight case, to show her that the top section wasn't cameras at all, but a place to keep an elegant black notebook, with a matching black pen clipped to the elastic binding, black noise-cancelling headphones, a black eye mask and a small packet of jelly sweets.

He likes black and he has a sweet tooth then, Laura noted.

"I'll grab those bits out before I get in my seat, then stash the case in the overhead compartment and that'll be me set for both flights. Barring needing the bathroom and wanting to stretch my legs, I'll be pretty much sorted for the duration of each flight."

"Impressive. You've clearly done this before," she said. She liked that he seemed to have his shit together and that he took care of the little things.

"It's not my first rodeo." Dan kept his eyes on the coffee cup in his lap and died a little inside. *God Dan shut up! Now you really do sound like a knobhead.*

Laura pulled her small bag from the floor and opened it to reveal a book, a small pink travel pillow, a bottle of water and AirPods in a pink case.

Dan, glancing down, noting the book. *"Colours"*? I've heard about that. Is it good?"

"It's apparently one of those romance novels. You know where two people fall in love and it's obvious but it makes your heart hurt. I've only just started reading it but yeah, it lives up to the hype. Next time I bump into you in an airport I'll lend it to you." Smiling knowing that it would never happen, she turned her attention to her lack of eye mask.

"Maybe I should get an eye mask too? I was hoping to nap on the plane. Do you think I need one?" She probably didn't really need one but she was unsure and felt like the experienced traveller would know.

"Well I'm a social introvert," he said, averting his eyes as if on cue, 'so when I fly I like to shut myself away as much as I can. If you weren't planning to sleep, I'd say you'd probably be fine."

Laura looked from the coffee cup in her hands to the travel

shop behind her on the concourse and then back at Dan.

"There's no way this coffee is keeping me awake for the whole flight. Hold this please, I'll be back." She thrust her coffee cup into his free hand and made her way to the nearby shop which sold the usual expensive airport souvenirs that people thought they needed but usually didn't.

He watched her walk away and breathed for what felt like the first time in the last five minutes. He couldn't help but marvel at the weird twist of fate that she was in the same airport as him at exactly the same moment.

~

Dan's work had always kept him single. He'd had relationships from time to time throughout the years, but no one had really fitted into his life fully and eventually the relationships fizzled out to nothing and he'd moved on.

Being so invested in his work and his business, meant it was hard for him to commit fully to a partner. It was always going to be hard for anyone to feel a part of a relationship when the other person was thinking about work all the time. He knew that and how unfair it could be on others, so he resolved to not get romantically involved whenever possible. Work, travel and creating, were the things he loved. He was okay with that.

~

Laura scanned the cheapest eye mask she could find and paid the machine as it bleeped at her. She knew she probably wouldn't need it really but she was relieved to have an excuse to have a minute to herself. Sitting back at the gate with Dan, she'd felt comfortable with this man who was probably ten years her senior and this in turn had made her feel uncomfortable.

She hadn't seen him in so long and he'd been so nice to her the first time they'd met, trying to make her feel comfortable on set and in front of the camera, even though she had felt stressed all day.

Laura hadn't intentionally been in a one-on-one situation with a man since her break up with Chris. Aside from hugs with her dad when she was despondent about what future lay ahead of her, she'd had no physical contact with any other men. Anything else, with anybody else felt too hard and so she avoided it at all costs.

She knew she wasn't ready to date now, or if she ever would be again. Chris had just about devastated the 27-year-old professional rugby player, destroying their long-term relationship by sleeping with some woman he'd met at work.

To Laura, he was meant to be her happily ever after and finding out that he wasn't, had shattered her trust in men and wiped out her future plans in one fell swoop. Now as she picked up her unnecessary eye mask, she felt the same nervousness usually felt on a first date even though this wasn't even a date, they were only talking. She felt conspicuous.

Turning on her heel, she made her way back across the quiet concourse to Gate 9 and the waiting man who had made her smile. Dan watched her heading back to him. Seeing him watching her gave her a sense of unease, like she was on show. She was glad when he handed back her coffee, so she had something to do with her hands after dropping the eye mask on top of her bag. The cup was still warm but more from his touch than the milky liquid inside.

~

"Be careful, Laura."

Sarah Miller was Laura's team captain and oldest friend. Having played rugby at the same school as teenagers, the two women were lifelong friends and had played for the same club for the last six seasons.

The night she'd found out Chris was cheating on her, when it became obvious their relationship was over, it was Sarah that Laura had called first when all hope was lost.

She was the kind of person who called a spade a spade and it was one of the things Laura liked best about her friend. She would listen and tell you her opinion if you asked for it, but she'd not sugarcoat anything even if that's what the moment called for.

"What do you mean?" Laura tried to focus on the boarding pass and passport in her hand as she queued to get checked in at the gate. The line was moving painstakingly slowly and she knew that if she was in trouble, Sarah had the perfect opportunity to tell her about it, all but leaning over her shoulder.

Laura had finally met up with her friends after they'd purchased far too much duty-free and had raced to the gate with only minutes to spare.

"Be careful you don't end up enjoying yourself on this trip. Seems you're well on your way!"

Laura couldn't see her friend's face but she knew full well the 6'1" brunette would have a mischievous smile plastered across it.

"I thought that was the point? Wasn't that why you begged me to come away, against my better judgement?"

"Whoa, first of all, I didn't beg" retorted Sarah feigning indignation, "and secondly you know what I mean. You could have saved us some seats anywhere at the gate while we shopped, but instead, you find yourself sitting next to possibly the only eligible bachelor in the airport."

"Stop it..." Laura knew her friend was trying to get a rise out of her but she wasn't going to bite. Sarah could find someone else to tease for the trip.

"I'm just saying he's still cute, he's better looking in fact, and you could do with some happiness in your life after the shitshow you've had for the past few months."

Laura thought back to the last hour she'd spent with Dan, talking about his work and his travels. It was nice not to be the focus of attention for a change and whether he'd sensed that or not, the photographer had happily taken the time to talk about himself, keeping the conversation light and on him.

For sixty minutes she'd not felt as though she was broken and that all everyone wanted to do was ask her if she was okay. Dan hadn't asked her that. He'd just accepted she was there and that was enough. She felt, for want of a better word, normal again. But as soon as she considered it, waves of sadness rushed through her as she saw flashbacks from the past few months. The fight. Chris admitting what he'd done. Twisting her words until she didn't know fact from fiction. All the sleepless nights back at her parents' house wondering what she'd done so wrong to make him do that. Wondering if her heart would ever mend.

"I can't. Not this weekend." She said, swallowing hard, "It's too soon".

Sarah sensed she'd taken things too far and her friend wasn't ready for that kind of banter yet so reaching around, she pulled Laura into a bear hug with one of her strong arms and kissed her friend's cheek.

"I love you."

"I love you too" Laura replied as she handed the stewardess her boarding pass and made her way down the ramp onto the waiting plane.

You always hand over the good things first, here is my laughter, here is my confidence, here is the part of me I think is cute and worth loving. Eventually you close your eyes and hold out something heavy - here is the thing you might leave me for. If you're lucky, they pick it up easily. If you're lucky, they'll let you hold theirs too.

~ Rebeka Anne

Chapter 3

"I'm like a prisoner, captured in your eyes."

Dan sat in his Executive Class seat on the Boeing 787 Dreamliner bound for Rome Fiumicino Airport and stared out of the window somewhere over Europe, music playing in his noise-cancelling headphones. He'd spent the first hour of the flight trying to sleep but whenever he closed his eyes he just saw her face and replayed all their interactions from earlier that morning.

After a while, he'd given up trying to sleep. It was clear it wasn't happening anytime soon. Flicking through the movies available on the small in-flight entertainment screen in front of him, he'd tried to watch the latest blockbuster movie but it didn't seem to grab his attention quite as he'd hoped. Giving up, the 38-year-old turned it off, pulled up a playlist on his phone of his favourite blues artists and had taken to looking out of the window letting his mind wander.

"Sir?" The presence and distant voice of the stewardess pulled him out of his thoughts and made him jump. He shook his head a little and slipped off his headphones so he could hear her properly.

"Sorry, miles away."

"It's ok, Sir. I asked if you'd like anything to drink?"

"Oh, no I'm fine thank you."

Definitely too early to start sipping whiskey, no matter what time zone I'm in, he thought as the red-haired stewardess moved off down the cabin to the next passenger, as if she was selling her wares on the street moving from punter to punter.

Pushing his headphones back on, he tried to think ahead to the task at hand for the next few days.

As he sat and watched the clouds beneath him slide past, he visualised the sort of things he'd do over the coming days and the type of images he'd like to get. He'd already made some notes in his ever-present notepad but seeing them form in his mind's eye was an important part of his process.

Words and notes were fine, but nothing made up for the art of seeing an image before he took it. Years of experience had taught him that. It was important that as an artist, he trusted his instincts and then backed himself to get the images he wanted. Doing so, while letting his creativity flow, would always bring the special sort of images he wanted.

However, as he thought through his shots list, Dan's mind wandered to thoughts of Laura and how she'd look in certain images he had in mind for the project. *Don't be ridiculous,* he told himself.

~

Sitting further back in the cabin in her Economy seat, Laura sat alone. Being an early morning flight, some of the plane's seats were empty and she'd found herself lucky enough to have an unoccupied seat next to her as they took off. It wasn't quite the Executive Class seat that Dan had on the other side of the mythical curtain ahead of her, that separated the special people from the rest of the flight, but for the next few hours, it would do nicely.

He'd explained, as his group had been called early to board back at Heathrow, that flying so often afforded him the opportunity to upgrade from time to time and so when the ticket arrived in his inbox a few weeks before, he'd jumped at the chance. She wondered what it was like up there and what he'd be doing at this very moment.

Get it together Laura, for fuck's sake! She knew she shouldn't be wondering about him like that but a part of her consciousness couldn't stop herself.

She stabbed at the screen on the seat-back in front of her and found a movie to watch, relieved to have her attention on something else for a while. As scene after scene played, the plot became painfully obvious after only fifteen minutes. Girl meets boy. They fall in love. Boy and girl fight over something stupid. Boy makes some overly extravagant declaration of love. Girl forgives him and they live happily ever after.

Such rubbish, Laura thought, *He'll more than likely cheat on her in a few years when another younger, fitter girl shows up.* She turned it off and wondered if Dan was the sort of guy to cheat. That thought made her uncomfortable and she was determined she would never be in a position where she would find out. She could do friendly but that's all she was prepared to be and anyway, it's not as if she was likely to see him again. She resolved to not get her heart broken ever again.

"Any drinks or snacks, miss?" A red-headed air stewardess leant towards Laura with a smile.

Not actually wanting anything more than comfort, Laura looked up. "Do you have any chocolate?"

After a moment's brief discussion of the options, the stewardess moved on to the next passenger and Laura unwrapped her chocolate bar. Breaking off a piece, she put it in her mouth instinctively and without any thought, she found herself looking up towards the front of the plane and bit her lip.

You can't connect the dots looking forwards; you can only connect them looking backwards. So you have to trust that the dots will somehow connect in your future. You have to trust something – your gut, destiny, life, karma, whatever.

~ Steve Jobs

Chapter 4

"I know she ain't ready. She won't be for a while."

Laura looked over at Sarah in their twin room in the Hotel Ulivi e Palma and sighed. *How did she have so much confidence?*

Their 4-star hotel in the historic centre of Rome, half a mile from the Vatican, was plush and beautiful. In the two days since arriving, they'd done the whole touristy bit, taking in the sights and sounds of one of the top destinations in Europe. It was loud and bustling with activity, for what felt like twenty four hours a day. It was definitely an experience.

Laura had tried to throw herself fully into the time away with her friends to celebrate Emma's birthday but her heart wasn't truly in it. She just felt distracted the whole time by all the thoughts churning around in her head. The girls understood. They always did, so they didn't push Laura too hard when they could see she wasn't fully present.

Tonight, however, was Emma's actual birthday and that would mean dressing up and hitting the town.

She desperately wanted to enjoy herself and blow off some steam but as the hours of the day ticked passed she seemed to find the daemons battling for control in her mind harder to silence.

Looking over at Sarah who was straightening her hair, she felt an impending sense of dread. Her friend already looked amazing in a long black dress which clung to her curvy figure, stopping just short of her ankles. She looked, as she always did to Laura, stunning. With her height and stature, Sarah managed to turn heads everywhere she went. Had she not become a rugby player, she could have easily been a model. Her dark hair matched her dark eyes and when she laughed, Sarah could light up a room.

"You okay, babe?" Sarah asked, looking back into the room through the vanity mirror on the wall as she ran the straighteners through her hair.

"Mhmm," Laura replied, quickly looking away and busying herself with her make-up bag which was wholly unnecessary as she'd already done her make-up. Sitting perched on the edge of her bed, wrapped up in a big, fluffy hotel towel, she'd been putting off this moment for what felt like the entire day.

Laura hadn't dressed up in years, not since an awards evening' pre-Covid pandemic, for the league her rugby team played in. That night she'd gone with Chris and went out looking nice but hadn't overdone it. She knew if she'd gone all dressed up to the nines, her fiancé would have felt uncomfortable about it and she hadn't wanted to do that to him, so had kept her outfit reserved.

Now, looking at the black and purple fitted dress she was supposed to be getting into, she couldn't imagine herself looking nice in it. Emma had helped her pick it out earlier in the day at a fancy department store in the city and in the shop mirror it had looked okay. With Emma's encouragement, Laura felt like it might work.

~

"I'm not sure..." Laura faltered.

"Babe, it looks great - with heels and make-up you will be stunning. It's always better in full effect"

Emma had coaxed Laura into the purchase, keen for her friend to cheer up and have some fun.

~

However now, looking at the dress laid out on the bed Laura couldn't picture herself in it at all and the excitement for the night ahead was slowly draining away.

Even though Sarah was focused on doing her hair she could tell Laura was stalling. "Just try it on and see how you feel. It's okay to be nervous. But honestly, you'll look gorgeous in it, I promise."

Laura sighed. Sliding the dress on, she couldn't get it to sit right. It seemed to hang on her all wrong. And there's no way her ass looked that big in the store earlier! Sarah stood behind her, now unattached from her straighteners and helped Laura zip it up at the back.

"You look stunning, babe," she said, smiling brightly.

As Laura looked in the mirror she couldn't see that she looked breathtaking. The dress made her look classy and sexy but she just didn't see it. All she could see was what she felt. Fat. Unlike Sarah her belly wasn't flat or toned and the dress seemed to do nothing to help hide that. And the way it clung tightly to her thighs made her feel positively awful.

As a rugby player, covered in mud, wearing shorts and a form-hugging technical playing jersey she felt comfortable with her body. It was built to do a job. And she was damn good at it. Over the years as she rose through the professional ranks of the women's game, she'd worked hard to build a strong and powerful body that would win matches and trounce the opposition.

Ten years ago in a dress like this she knew she would have looked amazing. Now her body wasn't right for dresses. On a rugby pitch, it was fine but as she stood there gazing helplessly into the mirror, she hated being different. For the first time in so long she missed her old slim body.

"I don't look anything but fat, Sarah." Laura crossed her hands over herself in an attempt to cover her belly.

"Babe, you look gorgeous, the dress is amazing," Sarah was being honest but she knew it would sound fake to her friend's ears.

"You wear it then," Laura replied, looking away from the horror show she saw reflected back at her. Realising in an instant that she hadn't meant that to sound as harsh as it had, she looked back at Sarah with defeated expression. "Sorry. This is just hard."

Laura imagined Chris's reaction had she come downstairs at the home they'd shared, wearing a dress like this. He likely wouldn't have said anything much but the look of disappointment he would have given her would have been enough to tell her that even if she liked it, he didn't.

Sarah brushed her fingers through Laura's hair, letting it fall onto her shoulders

"You don't have to apologise. I know this is hard. But honestly you look gorgeous in it. You might even pull tonight if you let yourself relax." Sarah could see the anxiety in her friend's eyes. "But if you want to you can go in leggings and a top, that would be less figure hugging. But I honestly don't think you have anything to worry about. You look amazing."

~

Twenty minutes later they were in an Uber heading to a wine bar for Emma's birthday drinks. While she felt slightly more comfortable now, Laura was still trying hard to relax into the enjoyment the rest of her friends were feeling. She smoothed down her white top and watched the busy city and its bright lights sweep past from the taxi as her friends laughed and joked beside her.

Even though Sarah had gently protested, Laura had opted for black leggings and a strappy white top which flowed from her chest and didn't cling to her stomach. She felt nice in the outfit, but hidden and that was okay.

~

Arriving at the bar, the group settled into a booth with two bottles of white wine and four long-stemmed wine glasses.

"Here's to the birthday girl," Sarah shouted, raising her glass for a toast. "Here's to a night of fun and laughs and whatever trouble the night brings." The girls all chinked their glasses and laughed. Even Laura joined in, although it was more forced than her friends.

As the night flowed, the rest of the girls got up to dance and enjoy the music pumping on the small intimate dance floor. No sooner was she alone, than Laura spotted a tall dark haired man, in a tight white shirt, walking towards her table. She hoped he was just a waiter but her gut told her otherwise. Avoiding eye contact she kept her eyes on her friends and one hand over her wine glass. He was close now. Too close.

"May I buy you a drink?" The stranger drawled in a strong Italian accent.

"No thank you. I'm okay. I still have some wine left." She tried to kill the conversation quickly, she didn't like it.

"Are you here with your boyfriend or friends?" He was persistent, Laura had to give him that.

"Here with friends for their birthday but we're leaving soon." She kept her eyes on her friends, avoiding as much interaction with the man as possible.

"I think you're not leaving too soon though? Your friends are still dancing." He was charming but slimy. Laura's hands were trembling. She was desperate for her friends to come back so he'd just leave. She didn't reply.

"So let me buy you a drink while they dance?" The stranger had his prey in his sights and wasn't letting go, it seemed.

Thinking quickly, Laura formulated a plan and hoped her friends wouldn't hate her for it.

"Sure. I'll have another white wine please. I'm just going to the toilet and then I'll be back."

He smiled, flashing his pristine white teeth and headed to the bar, content to carry on his pursuit of the girl, who he now assumed was willing prey. But as he ordered the drinks, the stranger couldn't see that the hunt was over - his prey had already escaped, slipping quietly out of the booth and out of the bar altogether.

Laura jumped in the first taxi she saw as she stepped onto the street in the late summer evening.

So sorry. Was getting a bad headache so I'm going back to the hotel. Have a fun night. Love Laura x

She hoped her friends wouldn't be mad about the message sent to the group chat, but she knew she had to leave.

~

As she swiped the key card through the door lock of room 314, the tears were already forming in her eyes. She hated this. A part of her knew that not all guys were like that man in the bar, Dan hadn't been like that at all, but that part of her was being made to sit quietly in the corner of her mind while all her anxieties and fears raged through her like a wildfire.

Laura quickly discarded her top and leggings leaving them in a pile on the floor of the room, crumpled and abandoned like the night's hopes and dreams. She couldn't be in them anymore, they made her feel gross. Tears were rolling down her cheeks. She searched the room for a place to hide away from it all, the night, that man, her friends, her fears, her life. In her frustration she found it.

Locking the bathroom door behind her, she turned on the shower letting the steam build up in the small windowless room. Once out of her plain underwear, she stepped into the hot shower and let the tears flow with the water. Here she could cry and scream all she wanted. No-one would hear her.

She thought about the evening. How uncomfortable that awful Italian man had made her feel even just by trying to buy her a drink. She sobbed. her mind, as if trying to protect her, took her to a few days earlier when she'd sat with Dan sipping coffee in the airport. He'd made her feel safe and comfortable, which wasn't a feeling she was particularly used to. Dan's smile had made her smile.

Laura thought about how her life had gone to shit in recent months. She was trying so hard to put the pieces back together with help from family and friends but she felt like she couldn't make sense of it all. It was as if she was surrounded by smashed plates and bowls, unable to find where to begin in putting them back together. Laura held herself in the shower and let the hot water carry her tears away. A part of her wished she could just be washed away with them.

Stepping out of the small bathroom twenty minutes later wrapped in a big towel, she caught a glimpse of her appearance in the mirror. All she could see reflected back at her was exactly how she felt, a broken mess that no one could possibly love. She so badly wanted someone to love her and take all this pain away. *Why am I so unlovable?* She thought as she pulled on an oversized t-shirt and climbed into bed, her hair still wet from standing in the shower.

Her brain kept replaying memories of Dan, his piercing blue eyes, his soft smile, the dark tattoos that littered his forearms. Rather than something to flee from, she felt drawn to his safety.

The night dragged on, hours passed and she just lay in the dark, her thoughts churning. The room lock clicked and she heard Sarah whispering a drunken goodnight to the other girls. Laura quickly shut her eyes and feigned sleep. She could face questions in the morning, if and when she was ready. Right now she just wanted it all to go away and for sleep to take her.

I have this strange feeling that I'm not myself any more. It's hard to put into words, but I guess it's like I was fast asleep, and someone came, disassembled me, and hurriedly put me back together again. That sort of feeling.

~Haruki Murakami

Chapter 5

"I wanna dance with somebody. With somebody who loves me"

Chloe fluttered her eyelashes at him as his camera clicked away. Partly because she knew it was her job and she'd look great doing it in the photos; partly because she'd always had a thing for older guys with salt and pepper hair. They always knew just how to push her buttons.

Playing up to the camera, not caring about the fact the room was full of other people there for the shoot, she started to really turn up the heat. She knew what she wanted when this shoot was done and she'd done this more than once in her modelling career to get it.

God he's fit. She ogled his bare arms and hands, covered in delicious black tattoo ink. His beard was just the right length to scratch her neck as he kissed her, as well as other places too. She wanted to eat him alive.

"Jesus, Chloe!" Melanie Fisher was the PR rep for Exit Clothing, the sports brand for this particular shoot in Istanbul and she could see exactly what the model was doing. "Can we dial it back a bit please? Trying to sell yoga leggings here, not promote your OnlyFans!"

She knew the model was hellishly attractive but the notches of photographers on her bed posts weren't a secret in the industry and she really needed Chloe to keep it in her pants for this one. Dan Muir was well-respected and came highly recommended, just the sort of photographer Exit wanted for their brand. There could be no fuck ups.

"Let's take a few minutes," Dan said, handing his assistant a memory card from his Sony camera, wanting to take the heat out of the situation for a moment. "James, can you import these please and we can work off a new card for a bit?" Melanie pulled Dan to one side and she began to apologise.

"I'm really sorry. Chloe just gets…a bit carried away," she said desperately trying to keep the photographer on side.

"Melanie, relax, it's fine. It's certainly not something I haven't had to deal with before. We'll just let her have a little break and then go again. Don't panic." He tried to keep his client calm. He knew what he was doing. Younger, less experienced models could be like this sometimes; thinking he was their ticket to stardom. He wasn't.

He thought back to shy, quiet Laura, remembering when she had stood in front of his camera. She had such a gentle beauty it made his chest hurt, he could have photographed her all day. But like many beautiful things, the glimpse of her was fleeting and left him wanting more.

~

An hour later, they wrapped for lunch and Dan sat working through some emails on his laptop as he ate.

"So." Chloe started, sliding along the bench seat towards him. "Tell me about your tattoos." Her voice dripped with a sensuality she didn't have the experience or maturity to control, like a kid with a powerful water hose being flung around the garden, desperately out of control.

"Ah, they're just different bits and pieces." Covering his arms a little, not offering any more information, he carried on replying to his emails.

She giggled. "I like them. Do you have any more under there?" She nodded to his tight black T-shirt.

"No. Just one on my leg." He made no effort to show her. That giggle escaped her again, planned, rehearsed and delivered on cue.

"So mysterious." She slid herself away like a stalking cat and decided to try her charms on him after the shoot. She knew he wouldn't be able to resist her once he got her unwrapped. No guy could.

~

Dan hit send on the email a little harder than he intended and closed the lid of his MacBook, taking a bite from the sandwich he'd half-eaten during the break. Laura's face surfaced in his head and he wished he could talk to her.

He picked up his phone and opened his social media, clicking through to Laura's profile. Her avatar showed her smiling face. He needed that hit. Coffee and the blonde girl could easily become his drugs of choice and he knew it. Pining to see her even if only through his phone, he scrolled for a moment before becoming annoyed, he closed the app. Feeling like a stalker wasn't how he wanted to spend his downtime, but he missed her face.

In his line of work, he was used to being around beautiful people but the grip Laura had on his heart which she knew nothing of, meant he couldn't see anyone else. He didn't want to. He smiled thinking about how sweet and gracious she'd been on that photoshoot. Such a contrast to today's model.

Pulling himself from wondering what Laura would be doing now, he looked across the set in front of him. James was talking to the intern with the glasses and Melanie was having a stern word with her exuberant model. Dan just wanted to be taken back to the airport earlier that week, where despite the awful hour and the terrible coffee, the company more than made up for all of that.

~

By the end of the afternoon, Dan's head hurt from staring through his camera's eyepiece all day whilst simultaneously trying to keep his horned up model on task. They had all the shots they needed, using a variety of different sets and yoga outfits and Melanie was really happy with what she was seeing on the display screens. He had had enough of the model for one day, however, and was glad it was over.

"Thanks Dan. That was exactly what we wanted and more. You've knocked this out of the park today," Melanie said as they swiped through the images together on the big screen.

"Thanks, glad you like them." He hated this level of scrutiny, never knowing what to say in this situation.

~

"Fancy buying me a drink, Mr Photographer?" Chloe stood in Dan's personal space, flashing him a smile that she knew would end up with him grunting and her feeling like she could conquer the world, later that night.

"Ah sorry, Chloe. I don't mix business with pleasure." *That was a damned lie and he knew it.* "But thanks for today," he replied, stopping this before it got going.

"Awww! Not even for little, old me?" She was turning the charm all the way up to eleven and walking her fingers slowly up his chest. It didn't matter that he was probably old enough to be her dad. She knew what she wanted.

"Thanks. But no." He was direct and didn't want to mislead her.

"You're missing out," she smiled, stepping even closer.

"I'm sure, but to be honest, there's someone back home and she's all I could ever want." He wished it was more than half a truth based only in hope.

"Fine. Your loss!" And with that Chloe was gone, stomping off set like a child who'd been told no story before bedtime. *I'll take it as a win actually.*

Melanie stood awkwardly nearby. "Sorry Dan. We'll not use her next time. The models for the next few days are much more professional. Promise."

He smiled. "It's fine, honestly."

"I'm guessing that happens a lot? Your girlfriend must have the patience of a saint." She relaxed a bit seeing that he wasn't at all annoyed.

"Oh, Dan's single. He's just got a huge crush on someone who doesn't even know he exists." James appeared as if from nowhere, smiling because he'd just scored a point which he rarely got the chance to do.

Dan blushed furiously. "James, later this week when we're back in the UK, let me book some time in with you to talk about boundaries!"

Melanie and James laughed together, while Dan was relieved that Laura at the very least did know he existed.

CHAPTER 5

Isn't it funny how day by day nothing changes but when you look back everything is different?

~ C.S. Lewis

Chapter 6

" Take all your big plans and break them. This is bound to take a while"

Trying to figure out what she'd have, Laura scanned the board at the back of the shop. She wasn't in the mood for her usual skinny latte this morning, something in her wanted to try something different, but what that was, she wasn't sure. Decision paralysis. The doorbell chimed behind her and she knew any second now she'd be keeping another customer waiting.

"Oh I don't know," she said anxiously to the person behind the counter, who smiled politely and waited for her to make up her mind.

"Endo, why don't you make this lady one of your traditional macchiatos?" The man behind her spoke and she knew the voice immediately.

Laura turned to find Dan, standing behind her, black notebook in hand. He slipped his sunglasses off and hooked them on the collar of his black t-shirt. *Were they RayBans?* she wondered, looking up at him with a smile.

"Hello."

"Hey you." He held her gaze for a moment. "The macchiato is good here. Endo makes it properly."

"One of those please," Laura asked the small Japanese man behind the counter who Dan obviously knew. *So he comes here regularly then?*

Endo got to work making Laura's coffee while she turned back to Dan. "Come here often? Or is this payback for me surprising you at Heathrow the other week?"

"Dakuburedno is one of my favourite coffee shops and I've been coming here for years. And this is actually twice that you've pleasantly surprised me. First in Heathrow and now here. I didn't expect to see you here today." Dan smiled at her, trying not to stare.

"Well, this is my first time here. I had to come into town for a meeting and saw this place so I thought I'd grab a drink while I had a few minutes to spare." She could feel him looking at her, it wasn't awkward but she felt guilty regardless. That feeling never seemed to want to leave her alone, even though she had nothing to feel guilty about. Not any more.

The Japanese barista slid a beautifully crafted coffee in a small glass over the counter to Laura.

"I'll get this. Endo, can I have my usual please and put this lady's drink on my bill?" Dan said, taking control before Laura had a chance to reach for her purse. "My treat," he added, as she looked back at him concerned.

"Dan, that's very nice but you really don't have to." It was a lovely offer, but she still wasn't used to being treated so thoughtfully. Things like that felt alien.

"You're welcome," he said, trying to hold back his growing

anxiety about being around her. *Keep it cool Dan!* He reminded himself. "Would you like to sit with me for a bit? Or would you rather drink alone before your meeting?"

Her anxiety flared; she felt like she was drowning, gasping for air. "Erm...." She tried to find her words as her mind scrambled trying to cling to something. *Laura, get a grip! It's coffee. He's nice. Relax!* Her inner dialogue won this one and she took a little breath. "Yeah ok then. Thank you."

"Why don't you find somewhere to sit and I'll grab my coffee and come join you? I just need to talk to Endo about something quickly." He said, swatting away butterflies that seemed to want to consume his stomach.

~

A table for two felt too intimate, so finding a larger one for four near the counter, she watched as Dan briefly spoke to the barista and collected his coffee before joining her. Laura had placed her bag on the chair next to her forcing him to pick a seat opposite rather than next to her. She knew it was stupid and it would have been weird if he *had* sat himself down next to her but it was a habit she wasn't ready to let go of yet. Trust wasn't something she had. For anybody.

Pulling out the chair diagonally across from her, Dan put his notebook and coffee on the table in front of him before sitting. She noted how he'd chosen the seat furthest away from her and hoped it was a gesture of trying to give her space, because if it was she really appreciated it.

In a glass cup, with a small handle, sat Dan's rich black coffee, slightly bigger than her own. It had no milk but had a frothy top to it. As he poured in a single sugar and stirred, the creamy top seemed to blend in slightly to the drink before rising back to the surface again. Whatever it was, it looked delicious. His black notebook, which sat at a near-perfect right angle to his cup, was shut closed with a matching black elasticated band that was a part of the book and clipped into it was a black and silver pen. It didn't look expensive, but Laura felt somewhat that it was chosen for the job, rather than being a random selection.

"Thank you, Dan." She repeated herself but didn't know what else to say.

"You're welcome." He replied, "Endo does really good coffee. I hope you like it."

"I'm guessing by the fact that you have a tab, this is somewhere you come often?" *Shit Laura you literally asked him this two minutes ago!*

Dan chuckled, "Yeah at least once a week I'd say. Working in the studio is all well and good but sometimes I just like to get out and sit with my notebook and a coffee in a different space. I even get my coffee beans here for my machine at home. That's what I needed to talk to Endo about a moment ago."

"You have a studio?" She sounded a little surprised although she wasn't sure why. *He was a photographer. Wasn't that a given?*

"I do. Just outside of town. It's just a little space, but it's mine. You should come see it sometime." *You did not just say that Dan! Come on man!*

"Maybe," was all she said. Laura's insides were tensing. Dan seemed genuinely nice but her fears and doubts kept guard all the time. She nervously reached for her coffee and took a sip. It warmed her the moment it touched her lips. It was beautiful. Never a fan of very strong coffees, usually preferring something with lots of milk, she was taken aback with the softness and the myriad flavours of the small drink. "Wow" she said, her eyes wide.

"Endo has a knack of making perfect coffee every time. Not much of a superhero power I know but it's all he's got." He chuckled as he spoke, as though he knew how her brain was reacting to the liquid in her mouth.

"Wow!" She repeated.

"Like I said, it's his superpower." He smiled at her as he sipped his own coffee.

"What are you drinking?" Laura asked, her curiosity about coffee rising.

"This is a long black. It's basically espresso and a bit of hot water," he explained as he put his cup down. "You'll usually only find me drinking black coffee."

"I can't drink black coffee. It's too strong. Well, it usually is but this is strong and it's amazing." She was surprised by herself as she spoke.

"We'll make a coffee drinker of you yet." Dan said, half smiling, half trying not to look at her.

"If it's always this good, maybe we will." Laura said finishing her coffee.

"How was your girly weekend in Rome?" He asked, "did you have a nice time?"

Laura felt on the spot. She could be honest and tell him it had been really hard, or she could just say it was fine and bounce the conversation back to his work trip. She felt like some honesty was deserved; he didn't seem like a bad guy.

"It was okay. We had a nice time but I probably wasn't in the best mindset there if I'm honest. I went through a bad break-up at the start of the year so it was hard to get into the mood for partying and all that." Laura went silent. She hated talking about her break-up and she hadn't meant to mention it but for some reason the words just came tumbling out. Holding her hands together, she spun the silver ring on the finger on her right hand, and avoided Dan's gaze. Looking at the table in front of her, she held her breath and waited for the inevitable grilling about her failed relationship.

Dan paused for a moment, weighing up the options for conversation in his head. She hadn't intended to say anything about her break-up, he could see that written all over her face and he knew enough about what happened to understand that talking about it here in public wasn't appropriate. He changed tack.

"That's normal. Plus, I don't know about you but I'm not one for that kind of trip. It feels too *peopley* for want of a better word," he said gently, looking closely at the cup in his hand so she wouldn't feel on show.

She looked up. "Like there's too many people around and you can't catch your thoughts, when you'd rather be sitting somewhere quiet watching the world go by?"

"That's the one." Dan smiled but kept his eyes off her, trying to hide his own insecurities.

"That's how I felt! It was lovely being there with my friends and celebrating Emma's birthday, but there were just too many people. I'm not really into that any more." She could tell he understood and it was nice for someone to share the experience she'd been through, rather than try digging up her past. "How was your shoot in Turkey?" She asked, wanting to move the conversation back to him now.

"It was good. The clients are happy which is always a bonus but I'm not sure I was there long enough to work on the tan." Dan rolled his forearms as if to say, *"look no tan".*

Not wanting to look but still wanting to see, Laura glanced at his forearms, covered in black tattoos. Singular pieces containing words and phrases, like he'd grabbed a permanent marker and written down a quick reminder for another time. Something in her stomach fluttered.

Dan failed to mention that he'd been hit on by a model while away and had turned her down emphatically because since boarding his flight from Heathrow, Laura's face had been etched indelibly in his mind.

"When's your meeting?" He asked.

Checking her phone for the time, she replied, "oh in ten minutes actually. I should probably get going to be honest. Sorry." She smiled at him, feeling like she was leaving too soon.

"You have nothing to be sorry for. It was nice having a few minutes with you," he said, nodding a smile at her.

"It has been lovely, thank you."

Dan stood with her as she grabbed her bag and made to leave. From the inside of his notebook, he drew out a card and handed it to Laura.

"Would it be okay for you to have my number? If you ever want to see the studio, let me know," he said, hoping she didn't think he was too forward.

A sense of panic descended on her as she politely took the card knowing full well she wouldn't want to be alone with him in his studio. "Thank you, Dan and thanks again for the coffee. Maybe I'll give you a call sometime," she said, trying hard not to turn and rush out of the coffee shop.

"No pressure. But you have my number if you want to meet again." He saw the fear and uncertainty clouding her eyes and regretted mentioning seeing the studio, knowing that she'd seen it as a come-on which wasn't how he meant it at all.

Laura smiled and left, stuffing Dan's business card in the pocket of her bag. As she made her way to her meeting, the fresh air and freedom cleared her panicked mind. She needed to focus on her meeting, not the number written on the card which seemed to be burning a hole in her bag.

"Dan and Laura"

Laura: Hey, it's Laura. Just wanted to say thank you for the coffee yesterday. X

Dan: You're very welcome. I enjoyed the unexpected opportunity to spend some time with you again.

Laura: How much coffee is too much coffee by 9am? Asking for a friend.... x

Dan: There's no such quantitative measurement. You have to gauge it on how happy your soul feels!

Laura: That makes me feel slightly better....early start this morning. So tired. I think I'm becoming addicted to coffee now. x

Dan: Why don't you let me make you a coffee sometime, it'll be better than whatever you're drinking at home?

Laura: Thank you Dan. It's a lovely offer. But that feels like too much right now. I'm just not ready for that. I'm sorry. Hope you can understand.

Dan: The last thing I want is for you to feel uncomfortable. Of course I understand. How about we meet up for ice cream instead? I know a nice place in town.

Laura: Appealing to my love of ice cream now are we? x

Dan: WHO DOESN'T LOVE ICE CREAM????

Laura: Well I'm in town tomorrow afternoon to go to the bank. Barclays, near the square? Maybe we could meet at 1:30pm? For ice cream? X

Dan: I'd like that. See you then.

Chapter 7

"A love struck romeo, gonna serenade."

Laura Gray perched herself on a bench outside the bank and waited for Dan. Looking at her reflection in the window across the street in front of her, she pulled out her ponytail and shook her hair down. Hair up didn't seem fitting for the moment.

What the fuck Laura, she scolded herself for caring. It didn't matter if her hair was up or down. This was just ice-cream. She didn't want to get caught up in feelings, even though she wasn't having any. *Don't get carried away. You'll just get hurt.*

Taking out her phone, she checked the time again (like she'd done just two minutes earlier) and saw he still wasn't due to arrive for another five minutes. Her heart seemed to be beating a little faster than usual and it confused her.

As she tried to distract herself, she let her eyes wander across the scene in front of her. It was a little after lunch and the street was now mostly filled with shoppers going about their day, rather than office workers rushing out to grab a quick snack in between meetings.

A mother, engrossed in her phone, pushed a stroller slowly along the path in front of her, her toddler waving at everyone who passed. Something deep in Laura ached. She turned away.

An elderly couple stepped out of the nearby discount shop and shuffled across the street to her left, holding hands. She smiled. She wanted that. She wanted to be old and content with a partner she'd spent her life with, someone who knew and understood her deeply.

"You know, there's a fine line between people watching and outright staring."

Laura nearly jumped out of her skin. Whipping around she saw Dan standing behind her. Realising that he'd startled her, he quickly tried to backtrack.

"Shit! I'm so sorry! I didn't mean to make you jump. I don't think sometimes. Sorry." He looked sheepish and even though her heart was racing at a hundred and fifty beats a minute, Laura couldn't be mad at him. It was pretty funny.

"It's fine," she said smiling after taking a calming breath. "But you're buying me the biggest ice-cream they do to make it up to me."

~

"What would you like?" Dan queried as Laura looked through

the array of flavours sitting in their individual tubs behind the curved Perspex counter, five minutes later.

I'd have an easier time choosing shoes she told herself as the options in front of her seemed overwhelming.

"Erm…raspberry ripple please?" Laura asked.

When Dan got to the front of the queue he ordered a small single scoop tub of raspberry ripple for himself and a large raspberry based sundae for Laura. He even asked the server to stick an extra wafer in for good measure.

~

"Dan! Oh my God, I was joking!" Laura laughed minutes later as their ice creams were brought to their table outside the small ice-cream shop.

"I'm nothing if not a man of my word." He was chuckling to himself and she found it endearing.

The weather was warm and Laura struggled at first to contain the rapidly melting ice cream that threatened to ooze out, down the side of the sundae glass and onto the table in front of her. But she was no quitter and while she may have been a professional athlete, she also loved her food. This was a challenge she was happy to take on.

Dan watched her while she ate, her face full of glee. Not in a creepy way that would get him reported but in an interested, almost affectionate way. She genuinely intrigued him and even though he was far too anxious on the inside to do anything about it, Dan was content to just sit with her and watch her enjoy herself.

To Laura's credit, she finished the sundae and let the spoon ring in the glass when she finished. Although they'd spoken a little while they ate, there had been a comfortable silence that neither of them felt the need to interrupt.

"Thank you," she said, smiling and licking her lips. "You really didn't have to." Pausing, she added, "but it was delicious."

"You're welcome. Just remind me not to scare you next time. I'm not sure my accountant will let me put large volumes of ice-cream through my books regularly." Dan smiled but avoided her gaze.

She looked at him over the top of her sundae glass. "Expecting a call?" She asked, a little disappointed, as she watched Dan stroke the back of his downturned phone which sat on the table between them, small circles, round and round.

"No. Shit. Sorry." Realising what he was doing and how it was probably making the girl next him feel, Dan quickly put his phone in the front pocket of his jeans.

"My parents always said I was a fidget growing up. I always needed something to occupy my hands. This is the adult version and half the time I don't even know I'm doing it. Same thing if I have a glass of water with me. I'll sip it when I'm nervous and don't know what to do."

Laura nodded. She understood that incessant need to do something when she felt anxious. If she was feeling self-conscious or sad, she would often play with the silver ring on her right hand, twirling it around without really being aware of the action.

"I make you feel anxious?" She asked.

"No of course not! Well maybe. I don't know. If I'm honest, I wouldn't say I feel comfortable right now. Social stuff one on one like this isn't what I'm good at and I'm always worrying I'll say the wrong thing or end up boring the person I'm talking to."

Dan swallowed. Hoping that being honest and open wouldn't scare her off. He liked being there with her. He didn't want to be anywhere else but here right now.

"It's okay, Dan. I get it. Whenever we've met before I've been the same." She genuinely felt for him. "But I like the time we've had together and unless you have any pressing reservations, I'd like to spend more time with you." Laura could feel the anxiety flaring through her body. "If you want? Whenever we have the chance I mean." She was digging a hole and she knew it. "Not that I expect you to make time for me." *Abort Laura abort* she screamed at herself. "Sorry, now I'm rambling. What I meant to say is, next time the ice-cream is on me. Okay?"

Dan inwardly relaxed. She really was a lovely person. He wanted to sigh a long contented sigh but there was no way he'd be able to keep it quiet. She gave him an odd sense of being completely at peace while simultaneously being terrified to his core. It muddled him up.

Watching Dan smile a little half smile, Laura sat internally regretting opening her mouth. Why couldn't she have just left it at thank you instead of vomiting words out left, right and centre? Dan wasn't like other people. There was something about him she couldn't put her finger on. He was clearly attractive but not in a classic sense. She knew he was good looking but most of his attractiveness came from who he was, how he held himself and the passions he had. Laura felt muddled and wished there was some sort of handbook on this stuff.

"I'd like that," he said. "Well look" he continued, "I'm away next week. I'm travelling for work."

"Anywhere nice," she interrupted. *Oh my god, shut up Laura!*

"I'm actually out in Germany for a few days on a shoot. But I'll be back on Friday. Maybe I could text you when I get back?" He asked, hoping she would be ok with it.

"I'd like that."

"I'd say it was a date but it's just a text so not sure it can be classed as a date." *Dan seriously shut up you're ruining this!*

"It's fine. Text me when you're back and we can catch up." *Laura stop smiling. Jesus!*

~

Minutes later, Dan was walking Laura back to her car, her belly happily full of ice cream. The sun was shining and it felt like a really good day; every colour around them seemed to be lush and vibrant.

"So what's in Germany?" Laura asked as they walked.

"It's another brand shoot, this time on location in Hamburg. Have you ever been?" He said.

"No. I haven't travelled much to be honest." She had always loved the idea of travelling to fun new places but when she was with her ex Chris it was never something he wanted to do. If he wasn't working, he'd be at the football or out with his mates. Laura couldn't remember the last time she'd been on holiday.

"You should go. Hamburg is a beautiful place." *I wish I was taking you with me,* he thought quietly to himself.

Laura smiled. She imagined herself in Dan's company in different places around the world. She buried that thought deep as quickly as it had arrived at the front of her mind.

Sensing she was uncomfortable about something, the man moved the conversation away. "What about you? What's your week looking like next week?" He asked,

"Just training. It's the off season right now." He knew this but let her carry on. "So it's lots of base training and throwing weights around the gym while listening to music." The summer heat was working through to Laura's core under Dan's magnifying glass.

"Sounds a lot tougher than my job." Dan remarked thinking about how strong she would have to be to play eighty minutes of rugby. He hadn't been to a gym for a long time, preferring to run most days.

"It's just different, that's all." Laura tailed off.

He sensed something was off as the pair approached her car. "You know I'm probably going to text you as soon as I land, you know that right?" He said instantly regretting being so forward.

Laura smiled. "I'm not saying that would be a bad thing. When do you land?" She asked.

"Friday night. Around eleven-ish I think. It's one of those crappy evening flights where you hang around all day, you know?"

She didn't know but she understood what he meant. "Well I'll have to try to remember to check my phone before bed on Friday night then." She smiled as she unlocked and opened her car door.

"Bye, Dan," she said, as she got in.

"Bye, Laura."

He took a few steps backwards, not wanting to take his eyes off her for a second, then as she pulled away, spun on his heel and tried to walk away as calmly as he could, even though he felt like he could skip all the way to Hamburg if given the chance.

Dan and Laura

Dan: The traveller returns. Home but shattered. Hope my coffee machine made it back in one piece, I'm going to need it tomorrow.

Laura: Glad you're back safely. Please get some sleep. Goodnight Dan x

Chapter 8

"Swimming through sick lullabies"

Staring at the stickers on the chest of drawers in her childhood bedroom, Laura recoiled from the day and pulled the covers up over her head. Another year around the sun without anything much to show for it. As she lay in bed, she realised there was nothing happy about this birthday, it was going to be just another day where she tried to ignore the fact her life had gone to shit and she would have to just carry on regardless.

Her iPhone 13 vibrated on her nightstand and flapping the duvet off her face in frustration, she rolled over to pick it up. Scrolling through her notifications, mostly happy birthday messages from friends (which she ignored), she realised she couldn't hide in bed all day no matter how much she wanted to.

In a moment of sick desperation, she wished she was still with Chris; at least she'd be getting a birthday cuddle this morning. She shuddered, remembering that even a birthday cuddle wouldn't come without selfish demands. Chris was incapable of a selfless gesture.

Annoyed with herself and the day, Laura made her way downstairs in a sulk. When she reached the bottom step she took a deep breath and composed herself, knowing that her parents would be making a fuss for her birthday. Spending the day putting a brave face on was something she'd gotten used to.

"Happy birthday, honey!" Her mother chirped as she entered the kitchen. Laura smiled back.

Somehow, no matter what was going on in the world her mum always looked like she was ready to face the day. Sporting a green summer dress and complementary white cardigan, Emily Gray as always, looked nice. In stark contrast, Laura stood in front of her wearing an oversized old grey t-shirt and a pair of blue shorts she'd had for years. She felt a mess and probably looked no better.

"Thanks Mum," she said, crossing the floor to hug her mother.

"Happy birthday!" Her dad said over his shoulder, from the hob as he fried off some bacon.

"Thanks Dad."

"There's cards and presents on the table. Open them when you're ready. Tea?" Emily shot Dave a knowing look as their daughter sat at the table, while they carefully trod on eggshells around her.

"Please Mum, thanks. You don't have to, though, it's okay."

"Oh shhh it's your birthday." Her mother would always fuss given the slightest excuse, it was a skill set she loved to use whenever the chance arose.

Laura's father, Dave, dropped a plate into the spot in front of her at the table. You didn't need to look far to find where her love of food came from. While her mother was a fusser, her Dad liked nothing more than sharing and giving the gift of food. He tussled her hair as he moved back to the sink to soak the now used frying pan.

In front of Laura, sat a plate full of deliciousness. Three rashers of perfectly cooked bacon, still sizzling slightly following their recent exit from the pan. Two thick brown sausages, plump, their skins split slightly down the middle. A hash brown, so thick it could weigh down a tent in the wind. A dippy egg in a white egg cup, with the perfect amount of yoke trailing down the side over the rim. And her favourite, a slice of gloriously greasy fried bread cut up into little soldiers; just like he always used to make for her when she was little.

Laura knew that she couldn't eat her feelings away but she could shut them up for a few minutes and enjoy a birthday breakfast.

Her phone pinged with a birthday message from Sarah.

"Happy birthday babe! See you later at the gym. I'll bring your present then. Love you x"

Laura replied and went back to eating her breakfast while clearing the notifications on her phone. A part of her hoped to see a birthday greeting from Dan, but as far as she was aware, he didn't even know it was her birthday. She pushed the stupid birthday wish out of her mind with another mouthful of crispy hash brown.

~

An hour later, after a shower where she'd forgotten if she'd washed her hair or not, resulting in her washing it twice; Laura was packing her gym bag. However this was far from gentle. organised packing. Instead she was shoving sports bras and leggings in as though the holdall itself was at fault for all the frustrations of the morning.

"You know if you break that bag, you'll be even more annoyed than you are now."

Her dad's voice made her jump slightly but it pulled her out of her assault on the synthetic bag. She sighed and slumped her shoulders.

Leaning on the door frame with his arms crossed, Dave watched his daughter for a moment. She was still a little girl in his eyes but she'd been through so much this year already and he knew that she was shouldering a lot of troubles as a woman. Since bringing her to live back at home with him and her mother, they'd tried to help her work through everything but he knew that she had to do a lot of it for herself. It was part of being an adult.

"Not the birthday you were hoping for I guess." He said gently, not to make her feel guilty but wanting to sympathise.

"No, not really." She replied quietly, turning and sitting on the edge of the bed. "Sorry Dad. I'm really grateful for breakfast and my presents this morning."

"But?" He knew there was more to come and hoped by adding the *but* it would help her connect the thoughts she wanted to express.

"But," she began tentatively, "I didn't think I'd be back at home with my parents at 28, hating the life that I'm leading and mourning the loss of a relationship I should never have been a part of in the first place." The words connected themselves without her even having to try to make sense of them; it was as if her heart was speaking, rather than her mouth. "Sorry. I didn't mean it like that."

Dave sighed and went to sit with her on the bed, moving her haphazardly packed bag as he sat. "I know," he said, "but at least you're being honest with yourself finally."

"I just thought my life would be different by now," she said, casually spinning the silver ring on her right hand.

"You ended up with the wrong guy, Laura. None of us saw it coming and had we done, we would have stopped it before it started. It's not your fault.

I have never been more proud of you though, seeing you fight your way out of this."

"I don't feel like I have any fight left today, Dad." She felt exhausted, like she'd be battling for months, expending every ounce of her energy and it was still all for nothing.

"That's because you're near the end," he said quietly.

"What do you mean?" Laura asked, looking surprised at her father.

"When things are shit, they always feel the hardest right before they get better." Her dad never swore and on the rare occasions that he did, it was always out of earshot of his wife. "It won't seem like it to you because you're deep in this and you feel like you're done, but the reality is it means you're probably at the end of the fighting and things will start getting better soon.

I'm not saying the worst is over, but I do think you're near the end of this part now."

"You sound like a friend of mine," she said, choosing her words very carefully. "They're good with wise words like you."

"Ha!" Dave laughed. "Maybe I should meet this friend one day. I bet we'll get on like a house on fire."

Laura smiled, although the feelings usually associated with smiling didn't reach very far into her. "I'm so over feeling like this Dad. I just want my life to feel good again."

"It will, sweetie. You'll see." Dave knew it would be something she couldn't see for herself yet, but experience had taught him that the end was always preceded but the hardest fights.

"I should get to the gym. Sarah and the girls will be waiting for me." Laura stood and kissed her Dad on the forehead.

"When's your big media day meeting? Is that today?" Dave asked, trying to bring her back round to normal conversation.

"No, tomorrow. I have to leave early in the morning 'cos it's about an hour's drive to get there and I want to get parked up."

"Ah ok. I'll make you a tea for the road if you want?"

"Can I have a coffee instead please?" She asked, unsure why she'd want a coffee that early but she was developing more of a fondness for it.

"Sure thing. Go get to the gym. We'll see you later for dinner." Her dad smiled at her. She knew as long as she had him in her life, she really didn't need much else.

With a squeeze of his hand and an *I love you,* she headed out of her room to see her friends on her birthday, wishing it was just another normal day.

Dan and Laura

Laura: Was lovely to see you today. I didn't realise you'd be in the meeting. x

Dan: Yeah. Gemma from the comms team asked me a while back to get involved with next month's season launch. Was nice to catch up with you. Made my day.

Laura: You're easily pleased aren't you? x

Dan: I don't know what you mean Laura.....

Laura: Sure you don't smart guy x

Dan: So are you coming to the season launch media day then? Will I finally get you in front of my camera again?

Laura: I don't think so sadly. I think Sarah will come as captain. But it's exciting to see all the build up coming together. x

Dan: Devastated! I'll tell Gemma I don't want to be involved any more ;)

Laura: I mean why would you want to even be there if I'm not ;) x

Chapter 9

"That look in your eye girl, when you catch me staring"

In a conference suite outside town, Dan surveyed their handiwork and was relatively pleased. With his assistant James, he had spent the last hour unloading his large estate car and had constructed a pop-up studio at one end of the largest conference room. Now as he looked at the 3-meter grey studio background, twin side lights with coloured gels and the main key light with its large fifty six inch parabolic softbox, Dan was satisfied that it would do for the day.

James busied himself taping down cables and setting up the laptop they'd use to tether images during the session, allowing the client to see images as they were shot.

"All set?"

Dan turned to see Gemma, Head of Communications for the Barrett Women's Rugby League behind him, with her ever-present clipboard at the ready.

"Yup! All ready when you are," Dan replied. He was an old

hand at this so he knew even if he wasn't ready he could make it happen without anyone but James knowing there was an issue.

"Awesome." Gemma was nervous as she scanned down her itinerary for the day. "You'll have a player from each team to photograph and you'll have about twenty minutes with each. If you can do the basic headshots for us first, then when those are done feel free to get something more creative until we move onto the next player.

We have ten players today and they'll be cycling through photos with you, videography and some press interviews."

As she spoke she waved her hand vaguely around the room to show some of the different stations that had been set up for the season launch media day.

"No worries. Thanks Gemma. I reckon I'll need ten minutes max per player but twenty minutes each will allow time to play and show some of them the images we're getting on the screen."

Dan pointed to the laptop now ready and glowing on the stand next to his main light.

"Excellent, thanks - looking forward to it!" Gemma walked away anxiously to make sure the rest of the team was ready.

One of things that people liked about working with Dan was that he knew what he was doing and needed little to no input from them over initially telling him what they required.

The confidence he brought to his work, while not reflected elsewhere in his life, brought reassurance to his clients.

~

As player representatives from each team in the league started to arrive, James and Dan put down their coffees and got to work. The process was simple. A player would stand on their mark. Dan would shoot various headshots with them to be used for media graphics throughout the season. James would double check the images as they instantly transferred from the camera to the laptop.

If everything was fine, Dan would then shoot a couple of creative shots, adjusting the three lights of his portable studio setup via the small head unit attached to top of his camera. If they had time left over they'd show the player a few of the best shots and then mimic the process with the next player on their list.

Rinse and repeat until each of the ten players had visited his station.

~

Checking in with the member of the media team at the door of the conference suite, Laura spotted Dan working to one side of the room that was a hive of activity. When she'd been asked to stand in for Sarah, she'd known that he would be there taking the photos and she was looking forward to seeing him again.

Making her way to an empty table to wait, she made an effort to stay out of his line of vision. She wanted to surprise him. He would have no idea she would be there today and she didn't want him to see her quite yet.

Shrugging off her coat, she watched him work. He had an effortless air about him as he clicked each image; it was something she'd never really seen in anyone before and she found it fascinating.

Rather than his camera looking like a tool, it appeared to be an extension of his body, connected to his soul by his tattooed hand. He seemed to be completely in tune with his surroundings. Laura noticed that this effortlessness was putting the players he was photographing at ease as well, something she'd felt slightly for herself with him.

Dressed, as he usually was, in skinny jeans, black today, and a tightly fitting black t-shirt, he looked like he was doing what he was born to do.

She spotted his expensive-looking wristwatch, glinting in the lights shining down from the ceiling. It was the only thing on his person, with the exception of what was undoubtedly an expensive camera in his hand, that seemed to have any value. Laura felt that Dan wasn't one to show off with trinkets and finery. It wasn't his style and she liked that.

Engrossed in the show he was unwittingly putting on in front of her, she patiently waited her turn.

~

By the time it came to the sixth player Dan was in the groove, working with ease through each person in turn.

"I think I'm next."

He knew that voice, but he also knew she wasn't meant to be there that morning. He turned to see a smiling Laura standing off to one side, patiently waiting her turn.

"Hey! If it isn't my favourite rugby player. What are you doing here? I didn't realise you were down for this."

Dan was trying to hide his surprise and delight but he wasn't sure he was succeeding.

"Sarah was meant to come but she caught an elbow to the face in training yesterday. She has a beautiful black eye today to show for her troubles so didn't feel she was very camera ready." Laura was smiling and trying to control the happy butterflies in the pit of her stomach from being in Dan's presence again.

"Well," he said, "Sarah's loss is my gain. Come on. Let's get some photos of you."

As he walked her to the mark laid on the floor that kept the players all at the same distance from his camera when being photographed, Laura leaned in and said quietly, "Be nice. You know I hate my photo being taken."

Dan smiled and stepped back. "Trust me?"

Working Laura through the various shots he needed, Dan tried to calm himself and focus on the job at hand. It was all well and good being as excited as a kid on Christmas morning to be around her again but if the photos were shit, he'd be in trouble.

When it came to doing something more creative, he had her turn away slightly from him while he adjusted his main light to soften its effect on her face and smoothly turned the preview mode on his camera to black and white.

A few clicks later and he was done. Laura breathed and relaxed.

"James, can you check the batteries on the side lights please?" Dan asked, turning to Laura, "Want to come see?"

"Can I?" She seemed surprised.

"Of course. We're tethered today, so I'm sending images straight from my camera to the laptop." He pointed to the bright orange cable running out of his camera and connected into the side of his MacBook. "They're not edited but you can at least get a feel for what we're doing."

"I'd like that." Laura said as she moved closer to him and they huddled closely by the laptop screen.

First up were the shots he'd gotten to begin with, simple headshots that for years, Laura had been used to having taken. Even though they were basic, they were really professional looking. She was impressed, even though she knew she probably shouldn't be. Then Dan loaded up the last shot. In front of her, Laura saw a soft black and white photo of herself. She was looking down and away from the camera in a pose reminiscent of 1950s movie posters of famous actresses. The image made her gasp.

"Dan, that's beautiful. How did you do that?"

He wanted to say *it's 'cos I'm really good at what I do,* but not wishing to sound like a prize knobhead, said instead, "it's easy when you get the right person in front of your lens."

They were close enough together in front of the small screen that they could talk quietly. Almost too close.

"Thank you. I love it. You're very talented." Laura said smiling, delicately brushing her hair behind her ear.

Dan blushed and was awash with awkwardness. "I've got a break now, want a coffee?"

"Yeah ok. I have a few minutes I think." she replied.

Both of them were smiling like giddy schoolchildren and it even made James smile. *It was good to see Dan in a good place* he thought to himself.

Laura went back to the table to wait, while Dan went to the coffee machine outside the conference room to get them drinks. She pulled out her phone, reading a message from

Sarah.

Hope it's going ok. Thanks for stepping in last minute for me. I owe you one. X

It's ok. Just had my photos done with Dan. He's made me look wonderful. Going into a video interview next. X

Laura knew that her mentioning Dan would be enough to drive her best friend nuts and would encourage multiple messages and a barrage of questions she'd need to reply to later. She smiled at the thought.

~

As he walked back in with coffees, Dan's eyes searched the room for Laura, who was now being led away by Gemma through a connecting door to the video station, clearly on her way to be interviewed before it was time for her leave.

Spotting him, she grinned, holding her hands out in a "*what can I do, it's out of my hands*" gesture. He beamed back and stood awkwardly with a coffee in each hand watching her walk away.

"For me, boss?" James said as he arrived at Dan's side, taking a coffee out of his hand "Thanks!"

Dan chuckled and shook his head as he pulled out his phone.

You owe me a coffee date now you know?

I'd cut my soul
into a million
different pieces
just to form
a constellation
to light your way home.
I'd write love poems
to the parts of yourself
you can't stand.
I'd stand in the shadows
of your heart and tell you
I'm not afraid of your dark.

~Andrea Gibson

Chapter 10

"You could be the one who listens, to my deepest inquisitions"

"Ah, you made it." Dan smiled as he opened the door.

"Wow this is your studio? This is amazing." Stepping into the large open-plan space, Laura tried to take it all in. When he had invited her to see his studio a few days after he came back from Hamburg, she'd been nervous, but after talking with Sarah at length about it, she had decided to visit, just as an opportunity to learn more about him.

With her defences up, Laura felt that while she couldn't trust Dan, she knew that if she was ever going to move on from her past, that she couldn't hide at her parents' house forever. Sarah had told her she should go. So here she was.

As she looked around, she saw much that she wanted to question but the first thing she noticed was Dan with his hands in the pockets of his jeans, standing quietly beside her.

Glancing at him for a moment as he looked off awkwardly into his studio, she realised that this was a sacred place. And that being invited into it was special.

"Not many people come here do they?" She asked.

Dan stalled. "No. Aside from my assistant James, you're the first person to come here in probably two years."

"Why?" She asked gently.

Dan began to walk her into the middle of the studio. "This is my space. This is where I get to be me, where I can be myself, by myself. It's where I make and create, it's where I feel truly at home. And it's where I can hide." He added, looking down at the floor.

Laura suddenly understood the significance of being invited here. It wasn't a humble brag or to take advantage of her. It was Dan's way of opening up to her and showing her that he could be vulnerable. He always seemed so calm and assured, she didn't think vulnerability came easy to him. This kind of invitation wasn't given often, if ever. She understood.

"Thank you" she said, "may I?" And waved around the room as if to ask if she could explore.

"Mhmm," was the only confirmation he could give.

Laura made her way first to his large desk on her right. On top of the jet black desktop that came up high to the level of her chest, sat a large slick looking computer display screen, turned off for the time being. The matt black screen duly reflected the room behind her. Around the large display sat a normal looking keyboard and mouse, but what struck Laura was how clean and tidy it all was, although it didn't feel like he'd just tidied for her arrival. This was who he was. Everything looked like a surgical tray, all of it laid out for a specific purpose. A place for everything and everything in its place. She even noticed his ever-present notebook and pen that she'd seen him writing in previously.

Beside the screen sat Dan's open laptop. The slightly worn keys showed how much it was used and how important it was to him and his work. But it looked loved rather than used. She liked that.

In the corner of the room, Laura spied an acoustic guitar leaning gently against the wall, hidden slightly by the end of the standing desk.

"You play?" Laura asked.

"A little, but I'm not very good," Dan replied, his anxiety prickling. He felt exposed. Cutting her off before the inevitable, "I never play for people."

Laura just smiled and turned back to the middle of the studio. It was a large rectangular room with clean white brick walls. On one side were two large deep windows which flooded soft natural light into the room, both with low inviting window sills which looked perfect for sitting in and losing yourself.

On the far wall by the door to the hallway, was a large dark bookcase, fully stacked with books that, as a book lover herself, piqued her interest. Scanning around past the large black sofa and the low glass-topped coffee table, she spotted what she felt was a familiar sight even though she'd never set foot in here before.

On a sideboard behind the sofa was a metallic silver coffee machine, surrounded by what she assumed was tools for making coffee. It looked similar to a coffee shop setup, but like the desk, it was precise and meticulously placed.

She began by wandering over to the bookcase, with Dan not far behind her. As she searched through rows of books in front, she ran her fingers delicately across the spines.

"These are some of my favourite books. I read a lot but any books I don't enjoy, I tend to donate or sell. Everything else I keep and it ends up here. Nonfiction and fiction alike." She hadn't asked but he'd wanted to explain.

As Laura looked she realised that something didn't seem quite right with the books in front of her. Noticing her quizzical look, he chuckled behind her.

"They're arranged by colour rather than ordered by author."

Laura stepped back and she saw it. Each row of books was its own shade of the rainbow and seeing it as a whole she saw its beauty and its grace. It was different but it made perfect sense. She hadn't noticed it at first glance.

"Oh it's pretty," she smiled. *He's not like any guy I ever met,* she realised. "I feel like I could lose myself in these books and just sit here, reading all day." She looked longingly over at the large window sills.

"You're welcome anytime. As long as I'm here, you're always welcome," he replied softly.

"Do you have a favourite?" She asked, turning back to the array of books in front of her.

Dan smiled and reached over her to the blue shelf above her head. The movement brought him close to her for a fraction of a second, she could feel the warmth of his skin. As he gently pulled out a book, she turned to face him. He was close. The moment felt intimate without it being obvious or threatening.

"*A Fault in our Stars*." he said, holding out the book and smiling. "I don't have a singular favourite book, but this is definitely in my top five. It's a beautiful story. Here, you can take it."

As Laura accepted the book, her fingers brushed Dan's and her heart skipped.

Sensing her slight reservation as she looked at the cover, Dan explained. "It's a loan. Return it when you're done." She felt better for that. The idea of a gift made her feel uncomfortable, but knowing it was a loan relieved the internal angst she was feeling.

"I'll bring it back, I promise," resting her hand gently on the cover.

Carrying the book, Laura continued her sweep of Dan's studio. As she passed the sideboard, she was struck by how much it looked like a coffee shop.

"Will you judge me if I tell you my parents just have instant coffee at home and a kettle?" She genuinely worried he was going to look down on her for it and instantly regretted her honesty.

"Not even a little. Not everyone is as passionate about coffee as I am. Would you like one?" He asked, turning on the machine.

Laura liked that he was asking her for permission while simultaneously taking control.

"Please. Can you make one of those nice little ones that your friend, the coffee shop owner made?" she asked.

"A macchiato like Endo made for you? Of course." He smiled and got to work.

Laura expected Dan to do many things but she was surprised that the first thing he did was to place a small black set of digital scales in front of him as the machine warmed up. She watched intently as he weighed out a portion of light brown coffee beans into a pot he'd placed on top of the scale.

Seeing her curiosity Dan began to explain. "Making coffee is like baking. Yes, you can throw handfuls of ingredients into a bowl, mix them, bake it all in an oven and get a nice cake. But to get good cake every time, you have to follow a recipe. Making coffee," he explained as he emptied the beans into a hand grinder and started to work the handle, "is like baking. We follow recipes. Recipes that are created to work with different kinds of beans. So we weigh things and we time things."

Dan took the now ground beans and poured them into the metal portafilter and tamped it gently on the edge of the sideboard, "That way, we always get the same good coffee taste at the end."

Watching him talk passionately about making a coffee while working seemed to be intoxicating to Laura. There was something oddly attractive about listening to someone taking care over a process to create something beautiful that surprised her. He seemed full of surprises.

If her friends had ever asked her what her turns on were, Laura would never in a million years have told them it would be watching someone make coffee. But here she was, practically melting and it confused her.

Dan carefully let the shot of coffee run through into the cute little double-walled glass cup under the machine. never taking his eyes off the timer he had running. At exactly thirty four seconds he stopped the machine and removed the cup. It looked beautiful. If you were going to photograph the perfect double shot of espresso, this would be the ideal model. Laura felt like she almost needed to put her hand on the sideboard to catch her fall.

As he gently steamed a small jug of milk to finish off the drink, Laura's eyes drifted to one of the tattoos on his left arm.

"What does that say?" She asked without thinking.

Shutting off the milk steamer and quickly wiping it clean, Dan rolled his forearm out so she could see better. "This? This says *Go big or go home*. It's written in old Gaelic."

As Laura looked closely she could see it had been carefully handwritten and had clearly been done by an expert. And even though it was just black ink on Dan's skin, it looked beautiful. She wanted to run her fingers across the permanent marks, hoping she might feel his soul.

Dan carefully handed Laura her drink and smiled, saying "it's not quite instant and a kettle, but I hope it'll do."

God damn she thought to herself *this guy's good!*

"And the rest?" She asked, gesturing to the other small ink marks on his hands and forearms.

"They all exist for a reason," Dan replied, and proceeded to take a few moments to show her his assorted tattoos, explaining their meanings as he went. "What about you?" he asked as he finished.

"Erm, I just have one. I got it when I turned 19. My ex didn't like it, so I haven't ever had any more." She paused and her heart ached a little for what was lost.

Dan, not wanting to take her down a rabbit hole she wasn't ready to explore, simply asked, "what have you got?"

She put her coffee onto the sideboard next to her. Turning away from him, she gently pulled the left shoulder of her white t-shirt down. In the slow, easy movement that followed, she slid her hand under the strap of her sports bra, to fully expose her bare shoulder to the man standing behind her. She could feel her cheeks reddening as he stepped closer to look, feeling his warm breath on her skin.

On Laura's back, sitting above her left shoulder blade, Dan saw a tattoo, similar to the one on his forearm. No colours. Just a simple black cursive script. It read *Take a hold of your dream.*

The tattoo had left slight ridges where the needle had worked through her delicate skin and Dan wanted to reach out and softly trace his fingers over it. But he knew if he did, that he'd find himself kissing her neck as well.

"It's beautiful," he said after a moment, then walked back over to his desk.

Laura felt awkward as she covered herself up and watched him walk away. *Had she gone too far? She hadn't meant to.*

She was woken from her questioning thoughts by a familiar piano introduction playing from speakers that she couldn't see.

"Hey, that's my song!" She exclaimed.

Turning back to face her, Dan smiled. "I grew up listening to Paul Carrack, as my dad was a big Mike and the Mechanics fan. *Eyes of Blue* is one of my favourite songs. This live version is probably the best rendition I've come across.

Laura's self-doubt vanished. He hadn't been put off by her exposed shoulder at all, but had honed in on the meaning of her tattoo and was showing her that he understood. She smiled.

"It's my Dad's favourite song. He used to play it to me as a baby to help me go to sleep." She could feel the familiar hot churning in her throat that accompanied so many tears of late. She looked away.

Dan moved to her side, "I'm sorry," he said gently.

Laura took a deep calming breath and turned back to him. "No, it's ok. It's just a special song that's all." She smiled at him.

~

They spent a lazy afternoon together, talking about everything and nothing on Dan's sofa, until the street lights began to fill his studio with a soft orange glow. He didn't want her to leave and she didn't want to go.

She stood at the door as Dan told her, "seriously though Laura, you're welcome to come by any time. You don't even need to call. If you know I'm here, just come over. I'd love to see you."

As she turned to leave, Laura smiled; "You might regret that when I'm bothering you all the time Dan," whilst thinking *I see you in your safe space Dan, and I hope someday I can find the same level of peace and sanctuary.*

She found an easy comfort
With him for the way he
Soothed her mind. Effortless
Communication was her
Weakness and whether he knew
It or not, her thoughts
Pondered and then drifted
Away with his words in a
Cerebral dance. They were
Poetic and made love to her
Before his hands ever
Touched her.

~JmStorm

Chapter 11

"I'm caught up in this moment, caught up in your smile."

"So we gonna talk about it or just throw weights around for the rest of the session?" Sarah asked, dropping the 20kg dumbbells as gently as she could on the gym floor and gulping down a mouthful of protein shake from the beaker she'd left at her feet.

She'd been lifting with Laura for the past thirty five minutes, going through the session they'd been set by their S&C coach, and was dying to know the gossip her friend had to spill, but Laura wasn't giving anything up.

"We hung out. It was nice." She replied with a smirk that betrayed the vast amount of detail she wanted to share.

"Fuck! Off!" Sarah laughed. "Stop pussyfooting around it and tell me everything! I'm dying here!"

Laura, leant on the bar she'd just been using to do a set of squats and stopped trying to hide her smile. It ran from ear to ear.

"It was really lovely, he's such a nice guy," she began. "You were right, it wasn't his intention to make a move on me; I don't know what I was worried about really. He was kind and gentle and wanted to spend his time listening to me. I'm not used to anything like that. I dunno. Once I'd realised why he'd invited me to see it, I just felt calm. His studio is basically his safe space, so it was like seeing a little part of him most people don't get to see."

"What changed your mind about going?" She asked, starting to see her friend light up recalling her non-date date.

"When I saw him at the media day, photographing the other players I realised he was alright, you know? He was so placid and patient with them that I knew it couldn't be an act. It's who he is. A man like that wouldn't be wanting to make moves so I felt that I could go and see more about him. He had me curious about his world." Laura remembered watching him work and how it had made her feel.

Sarah smiled. Her friend was finally finding a small piece of happiness after every dark moment she'd been through and it was glorious to see. "So it's a nice place?" She asked.

"It's loads bigger than I imagined." Laura said.

"That's what she said!" Sarah joked.

"Right! If you're going to be a dick about it, I'll go back to my squats!" Bantering with her friend was something Laura hadn't done in a while, she realised now how much she'd missed it. Sarah held her hands up in mock surrender.

"Sorry. Continue."

"So it's basically where he works and stuff but he loves books, you should see his book collection, Sarah! I felt like I could have spent the entire day there just reading. He's lent me one of his favourite books as well, *A Fault in our Stars*. It's beautiful,

I've already finished it. God, I cried so much! Erm what else? Oh he has a guitar which was kinda cool."

"Like your dad?" Sarah asked.

"Yeah but it's newer and a bit nicer by the looks of it. The whole place is really methodical. Like he seems to keep things tidy and organised too, which was nice."

"What? Like your dad?" Sarah asked, trying desperately not to laugh at her own mockery.

"Fuck off!" Laura laughed when she realised what her best friend was getting at. "He's just such a nice guy. He made me coffee. We talked about the tattoos we both have but he has loads compared to me. It was lovely. I've never had a male friend before but he feels different? Not what you'd expect an older guy to be like at all."

Sarah needed more, like a drug addict trying to get more hits of delicious gossip. "Right. Quick fire questions. Ready?"

Laura smiled and nodded, leaning still against the weight bar. "Go."

"Where does he live?"

"I dunno. We didn't talk about that to be honest." Laura shot back.

"What car does he drive?"

"Erm not sure. I think I've seen him in a big estate car but that might be his assistant's?" She had to think about that one.

"Friends? Family?" Sarah was trying to glean as much information as she could for the sheer fun of it.

"Didn't come up, he seems to be okay with keeping his own counsel." Laura wondered if she should have asked more questions.

"Shoes or trainers?"

"Trainers. But they're nice quality ones. I've seen him wearing different ones."

"How did he make you feel?" Sarah had her friend on a roll and knew slipping in this question would cause her to answer without engaging her brain.

"Wonderful." Laura's eyes widened as she realised what she'd said. It was true. That was how he made her feel. She laughed as Sarah smiled at her and she knew she'd given a little too much away.

Sarah could see the waves of unfamiliar happiness washing around her best friend. The past few months had been awful for Laura and as her oldest and closest friend, Sarah had spent countless days and nights listening while she cried and tried to mentally work through everything.

Sarah had seen her friend left raw and open; it had been heartbreaking. Theirs was and always had been an easy friendship, carved from years of time spent together; but the past few months had been hard for them both. For Laura, having to go through so much devastation in her life and for Sarah, desperately trying to hold it all together for her friend. Listening to her talk about Dan was like a breath of fresh air after months of hurt.

"So you like him?" Sarah asked tentatively.

"Not like that." Laura paused. She'd replied instinctively but as she considered her answer, she realised she didn't know what she thought; this was all new. "He's lovely but I don't need anything more than a friend right now. Anything else just feels too much to even think about right now."

"But he's cute right?"

Laura smiled. "Sarah, I've been through a tough break-up, I'm not blind. Yes he's cute."

Her best friend smirked. "I mean, it wouldn't be the worst thing if you spent more time with him? He's nice. He's easy on the eyes. You know there's probably a long line of girls tripping over themselves to beat you to it, don't you?" Sarah had no doubt that Dan had his admirers, even though he didn't strike her as the type to have a girl in every port. "I think the phrase silver fox springs to mind."

"Yes he's lovely." Laura replied, still smiling. "But I really don't want to get ahead of myself here Sarah. He's a friend and that's all."

"So you're not seeing him again soon?" Sarah asked, knowing full well if she said no, that she would probably be lying.

"Erm."

Sarah howled with laughter. "When and where?"

Laura blushed and spun herself around in the squat rack, placing her shoulders under the bar. "Next Thursday, after evening training. We're going to the cinema, for a late showing…as friends." Laughing, she began another set of squats.

The mark of a wild heart is living
out the paradox of love in our lives.
It's the ability to be tough and tender,
Excited and scared, brave and afraid –
All in the same moment.
It's showing up in our vulnerability
And our courage, being both fierce and kind.

~ *Brene Brown*

Chapter 12

"Look into my eyes. You will see what you mean to me."

"So how are we gonna do this?" James asked, as they sat on the sofa in Dan's studio, surrounded by mood boards and a client brief that seemed to overwhelm them.

"Well I think we start with the basics. Do what we can do easily first. Then when we're in a flow we can start to work through the harder stuff." Dan was tired, they'd been at it for hours. The shoot they had in the morning was a big one and he needed to be clear on what he was doing or it was all going to fall apart on him. But even as he tried to focus his mind, he couldn't escape the thought that he was seeing Laura in a few hours.

His assistant was sketching out a floor plan and lighting set-up on the pad of paper that rested on his lap, creating a to-do list on one side of the page as he went.

Since bringing James into the business the previous year, Dan had felt like he was more able to handle the demands of his growing schedule. It had been hard to let go of some of the control he had, such was the nature of the man, but the trade off had been worth it. James was not only a good assistant, managing the calendar, keeping kit maintained and in good working order; he was also a great editor (something that Dan loathed to do) and could anticipate what was needed on a shoot before his boss even needed to ask for it. It was a relationship born out of necessity but one that had clicked from the very beginning.

On James' part, he was just grateful to be learning from a world renowned photographer like Dan. Even though his employer wouldn't allude to it, he was highly sought after and widely respected as a master of his craft. But if you asked him he'd just shrug and say he wasn't anything special, such was his way. James liked that about Dan.

"No, put that key light back a bit. If it's that close, it'll feel too soft on the models' skin. We need it to be edgier." Dan said, pointing at the diagram his assistant was quickly sketching out. "If we use the big softbox and back it up we'll get a better shadow definition."

"Yup yup yup." James said, nodding frantically and scribbling away.

Dan checked his watch for the time. Still two hours before he needed to meet Laura at the cinema. The tickets he'd collected earlier that afternoon, sat next to his phone on the desk, ready to pick up when it was time to leave, along with a packet of his favourite sweets for them to share. Usually one to fully embrace the digital life, he felt there would be something nice about handing over actual paper tickets to the usher, and he hoped Laura would appreciate it. There was something about her that made him feel like she liked those simple little touches in life, and he was more than happy to do anything that would make her smile.

"Boss."

"Huh?" Dan refocused on James.

"You drifted off for a second. I said, do we just need the one backdrop?" James ruefully shook his head knowing that Dan had been lost in thought.

"Yeah, sorry James. Let's just pack the white one, should be fine."

An hour later, the pair had emptied the storage area of everything they'd need for the shoot the following day and had it laid out on the floor of the studio. James grabbed a step ladder and set it up on one edge of the spread out equipment.

"Is this really necessary?" Dan asked.

"You put me in charge of your social media marketing so let me do my thing. Flat lays like this are all the rage at the moment. It'll take two minutes." James hurried up the small step ladder and stretched his arm out as far as it would go, trying to get his phone as close to the centre of the photography equipment as he could. With a few clicks, he was satisfied he'd got a shot that could work.

Dan gave him a *for fucks sake* smile.

"Look, we lay your kit out anyway to see if we have everything right. Why not make some content out of it?" James winked and jumped off the little ladder, flicking it closed, holding the handle at the top and his foot pressed on the bottom step. It made a clanging sound as he did it.

"Can we move on?" Dan said, smiling at his charge.

"Yup!" James leant the metal ladder up against the studio

wall and clicked the picture on his phone to edit it, ready to post online. As he did, Dan's phone rang on the desk.

"Bit late for a call?" James said out loud.

"Yeah." Dan went over to the desk and picked up his phone. "It's Sarah. I wonder what she wants at this time?", clicking accept on the call.

"Hello?" He said tentatively.

"Hey Dan. It's Sarah - I'm really sorry to call you late. I still had your number from when we talked about working together earlier in the year. I hope it's okay to call?" She sounded panicky.

"That's alright Sarah, no worries. You okay?" He had a growing sense of unease. Something didn't feel right at all.

"Look, don't worry but Laura has been trapped in a ruck during training and she's hurt her neck. She's okay, but they need to take her for a scan at the hospital to be sure. She wanted me to let you know. She said you two had plans tonight. I didn't want you to think she'd forgotten or anything."

Dan felt sick, it was as if someone was boiling acid in his stomach. He put his free hand on the desk next to him to steady himself.

"She's okay, honestly. There's probably nothing to worry about."

The room was spinning.

"Okay. Thanks for letting me know. I hope she's okay. Can you let me know what they say at the hospital please?" He was detached. Lost in a world of numbness and confusion. She was hurt and the idea that he couldn't help her terrified him.

"Yeah of course. I'll drop you a message when I know anything if that's okay?" Sarah could tell he was rocked by it but what could she do?

"Thanks Sarah."

Dan hung up the call and stared at his phone for a moment. Knowing what he had to do, he grabbed his keys and headed for the door.

"James. Lock up for me, I need to go." He let the door slam behind him before the younger man could even answer.

You have to learn when to shut your fucking mouth, and open your arms. Love doesn't need to have all the answers, it just has to be there.

~ J. Warren Welch

Chapter 13

"Through the sleepless nights, through every endless day"

He raced into the hospital's main entrance and frantically searched the boards ahead of him trying to see Laura's ward listed. Finding it, he ran down the corridor and straight into a surprised doctor.

"Sir, you need to slow down!" He shouted as Dan raced off.

Dan had heard the words *hurt* and *hospital* and had rushed out of his studio, without pausing for thought. He had to get to her as quickly as he could, nothing else mattered. He'd pushed the limits of what was deemed acceptable driving on the roads but he'd made it through heavy traffic as the rain had poured down. Pulling into the hospital car park, his message alert sounded.

Sarah: *She's fine. Just bruised nerves. They want to keep her in overnight. They've put her on the ward they use for overnight patients.*

Dan knew where she was.

Rushing into the ward, he found the admissions board behind the nurses' station, spotted Laura's name listed next to Room D and made to go and see her.

"Sir!" A fierce little nurse stood in his way as he turned round. She had dyed red hair and she seemed like she wasn't the type to be messed with. "There's no visitors on the ward now, you need to leave."

"I'm here to see Laura Gray, I'm her friend. She's been hurt playing rugby. You need to let me see her. Please." Dan was on the verge of needing medical attention himself, so high was his heart rate.

"The ward is closed to visitors, sir. I'm sorry." She said, acting like she owned the place.

"No. I'm seeing her. And you're not standing in my way!" Dan said, in a raised but decisive voice.

"Sir, no!" She stepped into his path as he tried to make his way around her. "Unless you're immediate family, there's no way you're seeing any patient on this ward. I'll call security. You need to leave. Now!"

~

The standoff ensued and soon everyone on the ward knew what was happening, even Laura who was sitting up in bed in her room, a few feet away listening. Initially she'd heard the commotion and it had distracted her from her phone, where she had been writing a text to Dan to explain what had happened. It took her a moment to realise that the text was pointless as he had been the one who had burst onto the ward trying to find her.

Laura's initial reaction though was one of panic. Chris used to shout and was often rude to people when he didn't get his own way. Old fears threatened to rise to the surface. But as she listened she realised that Dan was just worried about her. He wasn't being rude, he was just trying to see her because he was concerned. Laura laid her head back gently on the pillow and wished the nurse would let him in.

~

Dan looked over the nurse's shoulder at the closed door to Room D, and his shoulders slumped.

"Please," he said quietly. "You have to let me see her. I'm out of my mind with worry."

The fierce looking nurse seemed to read the situation and softened slightly. This probably wasn't the first love-sick fool she'd had rushing onto her ward late in the evening.

"Who are you here to see?" She asked, eyeing him suspiciously.

"Laura Gray. Room D." He replied pointing over at the board next to them.

The nurse considered her options. On the one hand she could throw this nut job out of her ward and go back to her game of solitaire on her phone. Alternatively, she could relent to the loved-up puppy look in his eyes and let him see his friend.

"Fine. You've got five minutes and then I want you out. I'll be keeping my eye on you!" She said pulling a face and turned towards Laura's room, Dan in eager step behind her.

~

"You know this man?" The nurse asked as she opened the door.

"I do," Laura said, trying to disguise the bubbling happiness, which she attributed to the cocktail of painkillers she'd been given. She felt floaty.

Looking at Dan as he entered the room, the nurse issued a strict reminder. "Five minutes," she said, scowling.

"Thank you," he said as she closed the door behind him.

Laura leaned back against her pillow, propped up in her hospital bed. She'd been changed into a hospital gown and had been cleaned of the muddy training pitch as much as possible. Her training kit was folded neatly on a chair next to the bed and a paper cup of pills sat with a glass of water, on the table pulled across her bed. She was smiling at him.

"You didn't need to come. I was just texting you to let you know I'm fine," she said.

"Ah you know," Dan said trying to hide the shake in his voice, "I was in the neighbourhood and thought I'd pop in." The raging storm of anxiety that had sat in his chest since first hearing from Sarah was fading now he could see she actually was okay.

"Sure thing, smart guy." Laura chuckled, instantly wincing in pain from her bruised neck. "Okay, so don't make me laugh. Apparently that hurts."

Dan moved to the side of the bed and for a moment considered sitting on the edge of it next to her, before deciding that this would probably be too forward so instead moved her clothes from the orange plastic chair and sat on that.

"Sure thing. No jokes. Got it." He smiled, relieved to see she was ok.

"Did you get into trouble with the nurse?" She asked with a nervousness in her voice.

Dan placed his hand on hers gently so not to disturb the cannula that was dug into her skin, brushing his thumb over her fingers. Her hand felt soft and warm. He could hold it all day and never tire of how it felt.

It was the first time he'd touched her in a caring, almost intimate way and it oddly felt like home; he hoped she wouldn't pull away. "No, it's fine. I just rushed in and probably startled her. It's my fault. I just wanted to see you, that's all."

"Rushed in as you were in the neighbourhood?" Laura smiled at him, her head tilted slightly towards him as she looked through fuzzy eyes. He looked a little shiny.

"Yeah, something like that." He smiled back.

Dan knew that injuries were an occupational hazard for a professional rugby player, but seeing her there hurt, he realised the fragility of it all. He also knew though, if they were to keep being friends, he'd have to accept it; this was who she was and he wasn't about to try and change anything.

"I'll be out in the morning, they reckon and then probably only need about a week off from training. It's my own fault really, I wasn't paying full attention and got the wrong side of the ball when everyone piled over me. The doctor says I've just bruised a nerve and I should be fine. But fuck it'll hurt when these painkillers wear off. Do you think they'll let me keep them?" She smiled like she'd sunk half a bottle of wine.

"And I think we'll take these away from you for now." Dan laughed sliding the cup of pills out of her reach causing her to pout. "I'm glad you're okay though. Honestly I am." He smiled and she smiled back. "I think my time is nearly up though sadly" he added, conscious of the passage of time.

"Boooooo" Laura said, the drugs starting to really hit her hard, like a teenager with their first bottle of alcohol.

"Is there anything you need?" He asked as he rose from the ugly orange plastic chair he'd been sitting on.

"No," she happily sighed. "I think I'm okay. Thank you."

He let go of her hand and made to leave.

"Dan?" She asked quietly through sleepy eyes.

He turned, as he'd made it to the door and looked back.

"Yeah?"

"Thank you for being in the neighbourhood. "Laura closed her eyes and let the drug-induced sleep take her for a while.

Dan quietly closed the door to Room D and took a deep breath. She was okay and his world could keep spinning a while longer.

Putting his hands in his coat pockets, he sheepishly made his way over to the nurses' station, where the nurse who he'd argued with minutes before sat, with one eyebrow raised at him.

"I'm sorry," he said, "Laura means a lot to me and I let my emotions get the better of me. I'm sorry I was argumentative with you. I was at fault, not you."

The nurse accepted his apology. "It's okay. I understand. Thank you for apologising. If it makes you feel any better, she should be out of here tomorrow, probably after lunch so you'll be able to see her at home."

"Thank you," Dan said as he walked away from the desk. He made sure to drive home a little slower.

Dan and Laura

Laura: Thank you for coming to see me tonight. You really didn't need to. I'm sorry you got into trouble with the nurse because it wasn't visiting hours. x

Dan: I didn't want you to be on your own there and I needed to see if you were okay. Don't worry about the nurse. She was just pissed cos I rushed onto the ward. I apologised on my way out. I'm glad you're okay. Get some rest. x

Dan and Laura

Laura: Watcha doing? X

Dan: Hey you. I assumed you'd be asleep tbh given the time. Why are you awake now?

Laura: Can't get comfortable. You? x

Dan: Can't sleep. Thinking of you.

Laura: You can't sleep because you're thinking of me? Or you can't sleep and you're thinking about me? x

Dan: Ermmm....

Laura: You're too sweet sometimes do you know that? x

Dan: It's probably all the sweets I eat or it's the painkillers making your brain fuzzy.

Laura: Some things don't get fuzzy from painkillers. Gonna try and sleep again. x

Dan: Sweet dreams Laura x

Chapter 14

"Living on a fault line...till forever falls apart."

Boarding the team coach, Laura found herself a quiet seat alone as her teammates busily chatted away. She didn't feel much like talking, something felt off. She just wanted to listen to some music and shut the world out for a bit on the journey home.

Holding the cheap takeaway coffee in one cold hand, she hit start on a playlist on her phone with the other, her AirPods already in her ears by default. If people thought she was listening to something, they'd hopefully leave her alone. She needed that pretence right now. Dark clouds were drawing in her mind and she longed to just escape it all, somehow.

Even though she was back in training, her neck was still causing her trouble and was starting to create tension in her shoulders and right arm. She ached. Physically and emotionally.

As the bus pulled away and headed to the dual carriageway, *Groovy Kind of Love* began playing in her ears and she was instantly taken back to her dad spinning her around the living room, with Phil Collins singing in the background. As she let the memory play out in her head, Laura realised that it was Dan that was spinning her around. The thought panicked her and she quickly paused the song, trying to find a replacement from the playlist. She couldn't listen to that song today.

~

While she searched for an alternative song, Laura overheard two players in the seats behind her talking.

"Oh, check this out. Three things the perfect man will do." Hannah said.

"Right let's look then, this should be interesting." Abbie replied and they both chuckled. "1: He'll hold doors open for you. Well that's a given. 2: He's great in bed. Obviously. 3: He's calm in a crisis."

"I mean they're not wrong, are they?" Hannah said.

"No," Abbie replied, "but these TikTok things are so surface level. The perfect guy is more than that."

"Oh?" Her friend asked as Laura listened, curious to hear more.

"Well for one, he's got to be older. Older guys just have a different outlook on life. I can't be dealing with a boy who doesn't know who he is, far less what he wants. The perfect guy does all the neat touches too. Like carrying your bags, taking control of stuff like paying for food and coffee when we're out on dates."

"Ahhhhh to be treated to coffee rather than having to pay for a boy's lunch. That's the dream!" Hannah laughed openly.

Abbie continued, on a roll like a rock barreling down a slope. "I want a man who listens. One that understands me and my needs. Someone who puts me first, y'know, makes me a priority. Who is going to show me the same respect if I'm with him or if he's with his mates. A relationship that feels like it's us against the world and together we can do anything. He's always got my back but he'll let me know when I'm wrong. Someone I can laugh and cry with and not feel embarrassed about either of those. One that wants me as much in a hoodie and no makeup as he does when I've gone all out. Someone I can be myself with. Someone comfortable and comforting."

She drifted off into silence as she finished speaking and realised it had become a bit of a monologue.

In the seat in front of them, Laura slid down a fraction of an inch. It was hardly any movement at all but it spoke volumes about her need to hide away.

Listening to Abbie, she realised Dan was all those things and more. He had never judged her. Even when she was sad or happy, he'd just been there, welcoming it all. And he listened, *oh how he listens when I need him to.* Whenever they'd been together, he'd always made her feel like she was his only priority, making sure not to check his phone when he was with her; a simple act but something that she noticed and appreciated.

Dan had this uncanny knack for knowing what she needed even though they'd hardly spent any time with each other, *how did he know?* He had so many of the qualities that Molly had listed.

But rather than feeling reassured and comforted, Laura felt scared. Not because of who he was, she had been scared by

Chris so much in her life to date that she was certain Dan didn't scare her in any way, but rather she was scared of how his apparent perfection made her feel. She didn't want to be catching feelings for anyone, ever again.

The scars she carried, felt like they were too deep to ever heal, so the idea of being with another man, ever, felt impossible. But Dan made her feel something she hadn't expected. Seen. He had somehow seen her for who she was and had stayed. Broken parts and insecurities abound, Dan was still there in her mind's eye, with that little half smile he did whenever he was around her.

Her vulnerability in falling for him terrified Laura, so much so that her hand trembled, making the coffee she was holding perilously close to spilling.

~

Watching the world slide by as the bus closed in on its destination, Laura felt an internal struggle building inside her. The one person in her life that she wanted to run to right now, was becoming the sole source of her problems in their current form. She wanted to just see Dan because she knew he'd find the right thing to say to make it all better, but at the same time he would make her feel more and that felt dangerous.

~

Her phone rang. Seeing *Mum* on the caller ID, she accepted the call and looked out the window as she heard her mother's voice in her AirPods.

"Hey Mum," she said, composing herself.

"Hi honey. Your dad's taking me out for the night to see a show in town. So we might not be back till late." Her mother was talking at pace, clearly excited.

"Yeah okay. Sounds nice." Laura replied, feeling her stomach drop.

"Hang on. Here's your dad." Emily chuckled as she passed the phone to her husband.

"Hey sweetie. You gonna be okay tonight?" He asked.

"Yeah of course, Dad. I'm just tired."

"Ok well make sure you eat something when you get in please? Don't just go straight to bed." He knew what his daughter was like when she was tired. "Oh, and don't leave your keys in the door or we'll not be able to get back in."

"Sure thing, Dad. Have a nice time." Laura hung up. She wanted that. She wanted cute, random date nights with someone who gave a shit about her. Who wanted her for her and made her feel wanted.

She thought about Dan and what he'd told her.

Seriously though Laura, you're welcome to come by any time. You don't even need to call. If you know I'm here, just come over. I'd love to see you.

Deep down, she knew it was a bad idea. Resolving to just go home and go to bed, she watched as the car park came into view ahead.

~

Laura said her goodbyes to the team as they exited the bus and then went to her car.

I shouldn't see him. I should just go home and go to bed.

Laura pulled out her phone and opened her message app.

CHAPTER 14

"Dan and Laura"

September 26th 5:38pm

Laura: Hey. Are you in the studio tonight? x

Dan: Hey you. Yeah working on an edit. Why?

Laura: Mum and Dad are out and I've not had the best day. Could I come over? Sorry, if you'd rather not, it doesn't matter. x

Dan: Of course. You're always welcome, you know that. Come over when you're ready. I'm here whenever you need me. Have you eaten? Do you want me to order a Chinese?

Laura: Not eaten yet. But I should. Do you want to order it and I can pick it up on the way?

Dan: Sounds good, I'll send you the collection info in a second. x

Chapter 15

"It's not the storm before the calm. This is the deep and dying breath"

Laura knocked on the metal door to Dan's studio and instantly felt like she'd made a mistake. He didn't need this shit. He was busy working and she was just lonely and feeling sorry for herself. *This is a bad idea.*

The soft click of the door lock broke her away from her self pity for a moment but it didn't leave. It clung to her like the fog clings to the streets in autumn. But seeing Dan there, with that half smile, the one he did when he was happy but trying to seem cool, washed her with warmth.

"Hey you, come in," he said, stepping back to let her in.

"Hey, thank you. I just didn't want to be on my own tonight. But I promise, I'll not interrupt you if you need to work. I can just eat on the sofa or something while you work." She was rambling and she knew it.

Dan did what he always seemed to do. He stayed calm and

looked directly into her eyes to reassure her. He took the takeaway bag from her and held her hand gently, leading her further inside.

"Relax. Use this space as your own. If you want to eat then fall asleep on the sofa you can. You can sit with me. You can sit on your own. Whatever works, Laura. My safe space is yours for the night."

For fuck sake he's going to make me cry! Laura had been on edge all day and she couldn't figure out why. The bad day she'd had wasn't due to anything other than waking up feeling tense and anxious, like something was crawling under her skin. She took a deep breath and changed the subject to the food.

"Looks like you've ordered loads. I hope you're hungry," she said, twirling the silver ring on her finger as Dan unpacked the takeaway containers onto his work station. His big monitor displayed an image from a product shoot he'd done the day before. He was clearly in the middle of working. She felt guilty. "Sorry, you're busy."

He ignored the apology, excitedly saying "Ooooo they put in extra spring rolls! My favourite!"

"Hey! Mine too. Back off, smart guy." Laura laughed. *How the fuck did he do that!? She hadn't smiled all day, far less laughed.*

~

For the next forty-five minutes they ate and chatted while

Dan made adjustments to the images on the screen in front of him. He'd explained that most of the work had been done during the shoot the day before, so these images didn't need much editing.

He was just checking nothing was glaringly wrong with them and correcting any mistakes as he found them. He seemed so calm. Laura felt pangs of jealousy for his tranquility, as she struggled to control the brewing tempest that was on the periphery of her consciousness.

She tried to distract herself from the impending darkness and instead let her eyes roam around Dan's desk as she licked sweet and sour sauce from her thumb.

His work area was so simple and well thought out. Nothing was a distraction. Everything had a purpose. Her eyes fell on his familiar black notebook with its elasticated band and ever present pen, sitting in between them, by his right hand. Just seeing it there, felt comforting in some way.

~

"Dan?" She asked "what's in your notebook? I've seen you with it so many times and I have no idea what you use it for? Is it just notes and stuff?" She felt like she was intruding.

"Erm, well it's actually a place for lots of things," he said, placing his right hand on the cover as if to protect it.

Taking a deep breath, he pulled it towards him and carefully opened it. "So, sometimes it's for notes on photoshoots or from meetings I've had. I use it for jotting ideas down too. I keep quotes I like in here as well."

As he spoke, he flicked through the notebook so she could see the array of different things written on the pages,but never lingering on any one page for too long so as to keep its secrets. "And, erm, sometimes I use it to journal too." He spoke quietly.

"I didn't know you journaled," she said without thinking. It genuinely surprised her that he was so in touch with his emotions and yet as she processed that thought, it became clear that it really didn't surprise her at all.

Dan shrugged and joked, "not just a pretty face I guess."

God he is pretty though, in this evening light Laura mused.

"Have I ever ended up on those pages?"

"Erm yeah, actually. There's a journal entry from the morning we met in Heathrow. I wrote it on the plane as we flew out of the airport."

Laura was shocked.

He flicked back through the pages of his notebook, until he found what he was looking for and then began to nervously read aloud.

June 6th:

Bumped into Laura Gray this morning while waiting for my flight. Definitely hadn't expected to see her. Made me smile, although I probably sounded like a dick. She's as pretty as I remember her being.

"Aw Dan, that's so sweet." Laura sounded genuine but in her head she was falling into panic mode. Not because of his words but because of all the self-doubt that currently resided in her heart like a squatter refusing to leave.

Pretty? I'm not pretty! God, if he's got that wrong what else has he gotten wrong about me? What if I'm not what he expects? What if I let him down or disappoint him? He deserves a better friend than me. Everyone would be better off without me.

He closed his notebook and placed it gently back on his desk. He was just about to steal the last spring roll and return to his editing when he saw Laura's bottom lip trembling. A single tear rolled down her cheek and she screwed her eyes tightly shut.

"I'm sorry..." she started, but it was too late. One tear followed another and soon, she was engulfed in a sadness that was set to overwhelm her.

Dan rolled his work stool closer to Laura and wrapped her up in his arms. He didn't know what to say so he just pulled her close and let her cry, his hand softly stroking her back like he was soothing a child. He felt helpless and all he could think to do was be there for her and hope the tears would subside soon. It was heartbreaking.

"You don't have to be sorry," he said, actively having to stop himself from calling her baby.

She took a deep breath and slid her hand under his arm, looping it over his shoulder as the last of her tears fell. "Thank you," she whispered.

He reached out across the front of his desk and using the bag it came in as a tray, slid the last remaining spring roll over towards Laura. It was still warm and smelled delicious.

"Have the last one, I'm full." He said with a comforting smile.

Laura ate it but felt herself quivering, her emotions still bubbling on the surface.

"You okay?" Dan asked, concern in his voice.

"Yeah, just a bit shaky I think," she replied, trying to compose herself.

He thought for a moment, then rose from his stool, leaving Laura to look round, her gaze following him as he moved away. Opening a small box from beneath his coffee machine station, he poured a sachet of something powdery into a cup and boiled the kettle. Laura looked on curiously while rubbing her eyes.

A few minutes later, he was back, holding a steaming cup which he passed to her.

"Hot chocolate. It's good for a sugar boost when you feel a bit shaky. It'll make you feel better," he said fondly.

Laura looked up at him and knew he was trying to help and while it might not be working as well as he hoped, she was grateful that he was trying to fix something that he hadn't broken.

"Thank you," she said, taking the cup from him gratefully.

"It's just one of those sachet things. I bought a few for James a while back and he said they tasted like shit, so they've been left untouched under the coffee machine for a while now. They probably aren't as bad as he makes out though. James is quite particular."

As she sipped it, she could tell it wasn't the world's best hot chocolate, but sitting there with Dan in the evening light, as he looked at her with those caring eyes, she felt like it was perfect.

"I rather like it, Dan," she said, not looking at the cup, instead looking straight at him. Instantly regretting her words, she looked down. "The hot chocolate I mean," she added quietly.

Her mind was in free fall. She could feel a panic attack coming on and knew it was time for her to leave. Putting her half drunk cup down on the desk, she said her goodbyes and made excuses about early training the next day. She knew she was rushing away and Dan knew it too, but she had to leave. Now. He couldn't see her completely falling to pieces.

~

He really is a good guy. Laura thought as she drove home. But while her heart swelled slightly as she remembered his compassion, the dark parts of her subconscious still raged. She felt torn. All she wanted to do was sleep. Until it all went away. Her head fucking hurt.

Reaching the house, she ran up to her room and shut the door before tears engulfed her again. Mercifully her parents weren't home yet so her storming into the house and straight up to her room would go unnoticed and she could hide until the morning.

Laura got into bed without bothering to get undressed. She longed for the sweet darkness of sleep where she wouldn't feel sad anymore.

Whatever you want.

Tell me right now if I am disturbing you,
he said as he stepped inside my door,
and I'll leave at once.

You not only disturb me, I said,
you shatter my entire existence.
Welcome.

~Eeva Kilpi

Chapter 16

"What a wicked game you play, to make me feel this way"

The words reverberated in Laura's brain like a gong.

Well she's much prettier and thinner than you anyway.

Lying in bed at 3am, unable to sleep after yet another nightmare she sobbed gently into the night, her pillow wet under her cheek. Gone were the hysterical tears and screams that littered the first weeks after her break-up with Chris, but what replaced them felt much worse. The nightmares had started soon afterwards.

They were mostly dark flashbacks of their previous life together. Her subconscious trying to make sense of it all, according to the therapist she'd seen a few times after the break-up.

Tonight's dream had brought her back to the fight with Chris but instead of standing in their kitchen as she had done that night, she had been bound to a chair unable to escape as five iterations of Chris filled the room, taunting her and making her feel small. And then, just before she'd awoken they'd all become one and spoke the words that would now haunt her forever: *Well she's much prettier and thinner than you anyway.*

Laura screwed her eyes shut and sobbed. In the darkest region of her psyche a part of her wished that Chris had hit her that night. At least that way the bruises would have gone by now. Instead she was living with a wound that she knew would never heal, that only she and her best friend Sarah knew the whole truth of, the evil words that made her feel ashamed of who she was.

Laura's head was ringing, so she reached to her nightstand for a sip of water. The liquid was mercifully cool.

She hated how she now felt because of him. She hadn't seen what everyone else had apparently seen for so long. Why hadn't anyone said anything? Even as she asked herself that, she knew that in reality even if someone had said something she would've brushed it aside.

Laura knew now, that she'd been blind to so much. Chris's charm and charisma had slowly worked its magic on her for their whole relationship until he had full control of her. She felt ashamed of the person she had allowed herself to become because of him.

And she was tired of crying all the time. These moments of deep sadness and regret always caught her off guard after a period of doing so well. Only the night before, after sharing a takeaway with Dan at his studio, the tears had found her as she'd listened to him reading about her from his notebook.

One minute she was fine and the next, she was crying into his shoulder, her emotions in freefall. Dan had just let her cry and stroked her back gently. He didn't ask if she was okay or why she was crying. He'd just comforted her until the tears had passed and then offered her the last spring roll from the takeaway they'd shared, knowing they were her favourite.

Laura knew he was vaguely aware of what had happened but she wasn't certain how much he knew. He just seemed to understand without having to be told, which showed a level of emotional intelligence she wasn't used to having in her life.

It would not be a surprise if he knew plenty though. The break up with Chris had spread through the rumour mill of the rugby community like wildfire and as Dan worked on the fringes of the sport occasionally, it wouldn't take much for him to have heard about it.

Laura shuddered at the thought of all those people knowing the intimate details of their break-up.

The words *Well she's much prettier and thinner than you anyway,* seemed to haunt her. Maybe she wasn't enough. Maybe she needed to do better, be better. The idea made her feel sick. Laura thought about the way Dan sometimes looked at her, like she was the only woman in the room. He deserved more, better. It made her head hurt and her stomach churn. Maybe he'd be better off without me, she thought as she wiped a tear from her cheek.

~

3:49am. Laura desperately wanted to go back to sleep. She had a big training day ahead, she didn't need this. She reached for another sip of water. This time her hand bumped her phone slightly which activated its gesture awake feature and her home screen glowed in the darkness. Tucked between two other notifications about breaking news stories was a message notification from Dan. She stared at it but didn't pick up her phone. He'd be better off without me in his life, she thought.

Laura felt like everything was a mess. Everyone else seemed to have perfect little lives and yet here she was at 28, single and back living with her parents, in her childhood bedroom. She hated who she'd become. She hadn't noticed the change in her personality over the years. It had been slow and gradual to accommodate the version of her Chris wanted and manipulated her into becoming. It was, as he was, insidious. She rubbed her tired eyes with her balled fists, fighting off the words that lingered in the corner of her mind.

Right then, all she wanted was Dan. She didn't feel damaged when she was with him. She didn't understand why but broken was never how he made her feel. Laura didn't know what she felt. Everything was a muddle. *What was it about Dan that was different*? She didn't know but on some level, she feared that finding out could bring her a world of pain. One she wanted to avoid at all costs. Picking up her phone, she pressed the notification for his message.

Hope training goes well tomorrow. Thinking about coming to the game on Saturday if you'd like that? Might even bring you a spring roll.

Taking a deep breath, Laura swiped on the message and pressed delete. A tear fell as she saw her inbox now didn't have any references to the man she had exchanged messages with daily for the last few weeks.But Laura was certain she needed to keep Dan away. She didn't need anymore pain or hurt in her life and he'd be better off without her around anyway.

Like triage on the battlefield, she knew she had to cut off a limb now to save the body. Even though not being able to see and talk to him would hurt for a few days, she was adamant it was the right thing to do. To save herself. Dan would understand. He always did.

Placing her phone back on her nightstand face down, just like Dan did, Laura turned over and cried into the only dry part of her pillow left. She hated herself.

~

At 4:07am she finally fell asleep and dreamed of being held in arms belonging to someone whose face she couldn't see. There were no more voices now but she felt hollow, like she was missing a piece of herself.

in this world
so full of dark

she didn't want
to be saved
she wanted
to be seen

and among
the chaos

she didn't want
to be heard
she wanted
to be understood

~c.r. Elliott

Chapter 17

"you leave me defenceless"

Laura screamed internally and pounded her fists into the grass. *Fuck!* That was the third time she'd dropped the ball in the first half and the second knock on in as many minutes.

Twenty-seven minutes in and she was making mistakes all over the park. Every tackle she made slipped through her fingers. Every decision she made turned out wrong. And what made it worse, the harder she tried, the worse everything got.

Within the first ten minutes, she'd found herself flat on her back in the grass struggling to breathe as pain flared through her shoulder. Misjudging a tackle on a quickly advancing winger, Laura had gotten her head on the wrong side of the player she was trying to stop and crashed into the turf on her shoulder. It could have been much worse, she knew it. She'd been lucky not to go off for a head injury assessment. She should have seen it as an omen for the rest of the game.

Her teammates were quiet. She knew they blamed her but the team ethos was not to vocalise the blame for one another. Still, she could feel them looking at her.

Sarah hauled her up off the grass.

"Get your head in the game. You can do this." She snapped, jogging back into the line.

Laura tried to shake off the cloudiness in her head. She felt off balance and out of kilter. Her usual easy rhythm during a game had forsaken her and her team were paying dearly for it. They were two tries down and back on their own five meter line and she'd just knocked the ball on, handing possession back to the other team. *Why can't I do this?*

Play resumed, as the opposing team worked relentlessly to get more points on the board. Driving her painful shoulder into the gut of a player who was charging towards her on the line, Laura pushed up and back, smashing the player into the ground and disrupting the ball from her grasp and within Laura's reach. Feeling her teammates driving over the top of her to protect the ball, her scrum half pulled the ball from her hands and whipped it away down the line and off into safety. Pulling herself up off the grass, Laura breathed and was thankful her fuck up had been reversed.

They managed to hold out somehow till half time without conceding yet more points but they were taking a beating and they knew it. As Laura trudged off the field, the other girls avoided her eyes and briefly scanning the crowd, she couldn't see anyone she knew. She desperately wanted to see a friendly face around her. but there were none.

~

Sitting in the changing room at half time, she gulped down a sports drink and tried to not to lose control.

"Right ladies, we're better than this! We need to start building phases and stop giving away possession in stupid positions." The coach looked directly at Laura. It stung but she knew it was a fair point. She didn't say anything but tried to hold his accusing stare.

The rest of the team stayed quiet but she knew. She knew what they thought and what they were whispering to each other behind their hands and behind her back. The silence was deafening and she longed for it to end. She just wanted to scream.

"You okay?" Sarah asked, pulling her to one side as the team made their way out of the changing rooms to restart the match.

"I'm fine. Just let me do my job!" Laura hadn't meant for her reply to be so defensive but she couldn't help herself. Sarah just backed off with her hands up in surrender.

As the second half started, Laura tried to fight away the panic that was lodged in her chest and instead focus on the game but within two minutes she'd given away a penalty in their own half. The opposing fly half stepped up and slotted in three easy points, her side cheering triumphantly. Before play could even continue Laura was substituted. She'd run out of chances and spent the rest of the game sitting on the bench in her massively oversized dry robe staring out at the pitch, looking at nothing in particular. No one talked to her, not even the coaching staff. She just sat there drowning in her own fury and sadness, feeling alone.

~

Sarah came to join her as she stood on the pitch after the game while the teams shook hands in the growing gloom.

"You know if you need a week on the bench to sort your head out, I can speak to Coach. Let us help you."

"No!" Laura replied without even considering the answer. "Don't take this away from me!" Her bottom lip started to quiver and she felt a burning in her throat. "Please don't take this away from me," she repeated quietly.

Sarah pulled her into a hug. "We got you babe, don't worry. We just want what's best for you. Go home tonight and sleep. I mean really sleep. Use your rest day tomorrow to stay in bed and have a self-care day. This fog in your head will clear. You just need to give it some time. But we are all here for you."

She knew her friend was trying to help but Laura knew there was only so long and so many chances that she'd be given before she got benched. Permanently.

With a sick feeling of realisation, she resigned herself to the fact that rugby was all she had left. The rest of her life was broken and in pieces around her. The game she had grown up with, that had given her so much, was the only safe place that remained. But now, as she fought to hold back the tears on the cold, dark pitch, she could see that too starting to crumble around her.

"Dan and Laura"

[Laura's voicemail:]

Dan: *Hey. It's me. Look I don't know what's going on but I hope you're okay. If you don't want us to talk anymore that's okay, I don't understand why right now, but I'll give you space if you need it. Just let me know you're okay? I haven't heard from you in days. You have me worrying. I'm sorry if that's not my place but I can't seem to help it. Or myself. Laura, take care of yourself, please.*

If I never see you again
I will always carry you
inside
outside

on my fingertips
and at brain edges

and in centers
centers
of what I am
of what remains
~ Charles Bukowski

Chapter 18

"You wrecked my whole world when you came in, and hit me like a hurricane."

Martin France paid for two bottled beers and made his way back to the booth in the corner of the Wheatsheaf where his friend was waiting. The bar was quiet this early on in the evening so it gave the pair an opportunity to chat the shit and catch up. It had been a few months since they'd seen each other, as is often the case when you lead busy lives.

Martin was a Senior Designer for a large agency in London. Like Dan, his work took him all over the world and that shared experience allowed them both to understand each other better than most friends. Having worked together over a decade before when he'd been a print designer for the local paper, Martin had risen through the ranks in the design world and was now delivering keynote speeches at creativity conferences all over the globe, alongside the corporate work, his day job. They didn't always have time to catch up but whenever Martin was home from the big city, they tried to make the effort.

Tonight's catch up would be different to the usual affair however. Dan was hurting and Martin knew he needed to listen rather than talk.

"Still not heard from her?" He asked, placing the bottle of beer on the table in front of his friend.

"No mate. It's been a week now. Completely shut me out." Dan stared into his drink as he spoke.

"And you have no idea why? You're sure you didn't say or do anything wrong?"

"Not that I can think of, been trying to work it out all week. Everything was fine. Then nothing but static. She won't reply to any of my messages. Won't answer my calls. Nothing."

"That sucks man. I'm sorry."

"I know she's been through hell and not every week is easy for her, that break-up really fucked her up. She's had times when she's struggled before though but she's never completely shut me out. Initially, I thought something awful might have happened, but when I saw her share some stuff on social media I realised it was me, that I was the problem."

He forced a smile and raised his beer to his friend. "It's cool mate. My luck with women I guess. We keep moving forward."

Martin chinked his bottle on Dan's. "That we do, my friend. That, we do."

As Martin lowered his drink, glancing over Dan's shoulder, he spotted a group of girls entering the bar. He recognised the very distinctive looking Sarah immediately.

"So this Laura, she about 5'3", curvy, blonde hair, really pretty?" Martin asked while keeping one eye on the door.

"Yeah, why do you ask?"

"Well don't look now, but I think she just walked in with that Sarah we met once when we were out."

Dan whipped around. And as if his favourite photo had come to life and materialised in front of him, there was Laura with her friends ordering a drink at the bar. And without warning, seeing her hit him like a speeding freight train. She turned to look around the bar and her blue eyes locked onto his. He was a prisoner, trapped in her gaze, unable to move.

The electricity in the air was palpable. Everything around him disappeared in a heartbeat and for a moment it was just the two of them as the bar spun around them. But as soon as it had started, it was over and Laura drew her eyes away, making her way to a table with her friends, purposely positioning herself with her back to Dan and Martin.

Reluctantly, Dan went back to his drink. "Yeah, that's her."

"I can see why you're smitten mate! She's gorgeous." Martin couldn't help but smile at his lovestruck friend.

"I'm not smitten Martin, she's just a friend. Well, she was -

apparently not any more..." He paused and took a swig of his drink. "And yeah she is gorgeous."

~

An hour passed and the two friends had pretty much put the world to rights and were making to leave when they heard raised voices behind them.

"Fuck off Laura!"

Dan paused midway through zipping up his jacket. He didn't know whose voice that was but he didn't like the idea of anyone telling Laura to fuck off. As he turned, he saw her, tears filling her eyes, in front of a guy he had never seen before but instantly recognised. Chris Jones stood 6'2" and towered over his former fiancée. He was broadly built, with a dark thick beard to match his slicked back hair. He looked like a modern day Norseman. But he sounded like a prick.

As he watched, Dan saw a skinny brunette girl pulling the bigger man away and back to their group a few tables away. For ten seconds that seemed to last a lifetime, Laura stood alone holding back the tears before finally rushing out of the bar without looking back, not stopping to pick up her things.

By now, Sarah had heard the commotion and had started to make her way towards her friend and the main door of the bar. Seeing Dan heading in the same direction, and without the need for words, they both chased after Laura who was now long gone.

"Dude!" Martin tried calling after his friend but it was pointless.

~

Outside the bar, Dan took control. "Head into town and see if you can find her," he instructed Sarah. "I'll go and see if she's headed towards the taxi rank at the station and if I can't find her I'll loop back round and meet you in town."

Sarah agreed and was turning away when Dan called after her.

"Sarah? Find her. Please." Dan disappeared into the night.

Even though he'd sent Sarah heading into the town centre, Dan had an inkling that Laura would have gone somewhere quiet. As he walked quickly away from the bar, he came to a small shopping arcade. Aside from the street lights, it was in darkness as the shop owners had closed up for the day hours before; gone with them, any shoppers who might end up in this part of town. It was deserted and just the kind of place to run to if you wanted to be alone.

Then he saw her. Sat on a bench under a tree, hugging her knees to her chest. She looked fragile, like she could break at any moment. Dan's heart broke for her. He longed to take her away from this madness and look after her.

~

Sensing movement near her, Laura turned to see who was approaching.

"Please Dan. Just leave me alone". But he ignored the request and instead sat down, pulling her into him. She didn't resist.

The dam broke.

She couldn't hold back the tears anymore. They spilled over and emptied from her like a tidal wave. And while she cried into his jacket, a part of her felt safe, knowing that he had her and should her world and everything she believed to be true ever come crashing down around her again, he would always protect her. Those arms would always be there to hold her in her grief.

"I hate him," she whispered.

Dan just pulled her closer to him and kissed the top of her head, "I know."

"He makes me feel so small," Laura sobbed. Everything hurt. Chris had a way of doing that.

He whispered quietly, "you don't have to feel small any more."

For a while they sat, Dan holding her as her tears fell. There wasn't any need for words. It was simply enough for her to know that she wasn't alone.

After a while the tears slowed and Laura shivered.

"You're cold, we should get you back."

She didn't argue with him. She knew instinctively that he was looking after her and she trusted him to do that. They stood and she let him wrap her in his jacket. It felt warm and safe. Everything else outside of it felt hazy. But pulling Dan's jacket around her, Laura felt like she was able to go back to her friends. Something that seemed like an impossible notion moments ago.

~

Got her. I'll bring her back to the Wheatsheaf.

Dan quickly sent a text to Sarah, calling off the search and putting her mind at rest, as Laura zipped up his jacket for extra solace.

As they walked, he held her hand tenderly, never breaking contact, not even for a second, whereas Chris only ever touched her in public as a way of showing off his prize. He'd always been the same and she'd grown numb to it. This wasn't like that, there was no ownership, no bravado. This was different, Dan was simply showing her that she was safe. He was her way of staying in the moment and getting back safely. A lifeline in the dark.

Reaching the entrance to the bar, they saw Sarah just arriving and Martin waiting near the big bouncer, who looked anything but interested in the drama that had unfolded earlier.

"Oh my god! Laura, are you okay? I'm this close to walking back in there and punching Chris in the dick!" Sarah was livid and rushing around town looking for her friend hadn't calmed her mood any. The bouncer glanced at her and raised an inquisitive eyebrow. "Metaphorically," Sarah added with one eye on him.

Dan spoke. "Sarah, can you get Laura home for me? I don't think it best to stay now." She noted how detached he seemed, as if removing emotion from the situation allowed him to take charge and make sure everything was ok. He was a protector.

"Yeah, of course." She gently pulled her friend across into her arms. "Let's get you home hey?"

Laura just nodded.

"Thanks Sarah," he said.

"I'll call you tomorrow Dan. Thank you for finding her."

He forced a smile. Something he seemed to have done a lot during the last week or so. The night had turned chilly and at Dan's side, Martin was now rubbing his own arms for warmth.

"Wait! Your jacket." Before Laura could escape Sarah's arms to return the cosy protection, Dan gently put a hand on her arm.

"It's ok. Hang on to it. I can pick it up next week if you want."

Laura bit her lip and held back more tears.

"Thank you."

And with that they went their separate ways into the night.

The Beginning

Unconditional means without
conditions. Not I love you
but. Not I love you despite, even
though, regardless of,
notwithstanding. I love
you and that is the end of it.

I love you and that
is the beginning of it.

~Kristina Mahr

Chapter 19

"And she cried...Till the river ran dry."

"Dan? It's Sarah."

He picked up his phone before it even had a chance to fully ring. It had been less than twelve hours since he'd watched Sarah walk away comforting her best friend. While twelve hours is a long time to most, it felt like a lifetime to Dan. He'd barely slept, having returned to his place alone, around 10pm, where he sat with a half-empty bottle of Glen Moray Single Malt, playing over the events of the evening in his mind. Whenever he pictured Chris telling Laura to fuck off, he could feel an unfamiliar rage boiling inside his soul.

He wasn't a violent man and avoided confrontation at all costs, preferring to talk his way out of a situation but in the case of Chris Jones, Dan knew he'd happily do time in prison just to see that smug, self-satisfied look wiped off his face.

For hours he had sat, staring at nothing sipping a glass of whiskey. Just thinking. Thinking about Laura. *Where was she? Was she okay? Did she need him?* Probably not but he didn't know. He thought about finding her, hours earlier and holding her as she cried in the night. Most guys in that situation would have felt like a hero who had saved the day but Dan didn't. He just hurt. It hurt like dying from a thousand cuts that weakened his body and broke his soul.

Around 7am he'd woken cold and alone on the sofa, unsure when he'd fallen asleep. The pain and anger weren't gone. He checked his phone to see if either woman had messaged him but neither had, so making sure his ringer was switched on he got up to make coffee. Familiarity was what he needed right now.

As he started up his Espresso machine, his phone rang. He shut the coffee machine off instantly.

"Dan? It's Sarah." She sounded tired. He figured she'd probably not slept much either.

"Is Laura okay?" He had to know. Nothing else mattered right then. Social pleasantries could come later.

"She's okay. She's still asleep," Sarah replied. "She stayed with me last night. I spoke to her parents and told them she was going to crash at mine after a few too many glasses of wine. They don't suspect a thing I don't think."

The weight that had been crushing down on him for twelve hours lifted and he let out a deep breath. "Thank you."

“I think we need to talk. There’s some things you really need to know and understand.”

Forgetting about making coffee, Dan sat down on the arm of the sofa and listened. Sarah audibly took a deep breath, as if to prepare herself.

“Laura isn’t the same person you met a few years ago. Time has changed her more than you can imagine. When you first met us, she seemed happy. She was ready to get married, very much in love, hoping for a happy future. Or so we all thought. Behind closed doors she was miserable even if she hadn’t yet admitted that to herself.

Chris and Laura met at school. The whole high school sweethearts thing. She’s known nothing else, so her frame of reference on what love is meant to look like is hugely limited. She assumed for years that everything was usual.

But her relationship with Chris was anything but normal. As he became more manipulative and controlling, she told herself he was still the man she loved. He never hit her or anything like that but he would make her doubt herself. Chris wanted her to be small so he could feel like the big man and in doing so he made sure that she was completely wrapped up in him and she couldn’t break free.

You’d never know it to meet him in person but he’s a terrible excuse for a man. His outburst publicly last night was very rare and probably only happened because he couldn’t control Laura anymore.”

"What the fuck?!" Dan's blood was boiling. He couldn't think why anyone would want to do that to someone as perfect and lovely as Laura.

"Trust me I know. For a long time none of us knew. Then just after New Year, Chris came home from work later than normal. Laura questioned him about it and they got into a big fight. I am actually really proud of her for standing up for herself that night. Now I know the full truth of what was going on, the strength she showed that night is awe inspiring.

Chris snapped at her questioning him and told her that he'd slept with a woman from work behind her back. Made a sick point of making sure she knew how much thinner and prettier this other girl was. He really did a number on her with that. He wanted to wound her in a way that would never heal.

Laura tried to leave and he ended up begging her to stay in true Chris fashion by making her feel like she could never survive without him. So she stayed but she locked herself in the upstairs bathroom. That's when she called me and confessed everything.

Dan, I've never heard anyone that sad before. I could still cry now when I remember how her voice sounded on the phone that night. I could hear Chris in the background telling her she needed to stay, she was worthless without him and that's when I called her Dad as I couldn't convince her to leave.

I honestly believe had Dave not gone and got her that night, that they'd still be together now. But you don't mess with

Dave and while Chris is an arsehole, he's not stupid. When Dave finally convinced Laura to leave and went to get her, Chris didn't stand in his way."

Dan's anger had evaporated and in its place was a sad, empty feeling. Sarah continued as he listened on. He felt sick.

"What was left was a broken, battered and emotionally bruised girl. She was a mess. She couldn't sleep. Couldn't eat. And for a while wouldn't talk to anyone about it. Dan, I was so scared she'd lost herself entirely. She was back at the beginning without the will or the energy to start over again.

While she's now more like her normal self, she's not the same. She's all work now. Rugby is the only thing that makes her feel whole and even that's becoming a struggle. Everywhere else in life, she just feels inadequate. She doesn't know how she will trust anyone ever again."

Dan knew it was the truth. While he and Laura had laughed and joked together over the past few months, he saw the pain in her eyes and knew she still didn't really trust him.

"Look Dan, I know you two haven't spoken for a week or so. She told me last night on the way back here. You have to understand, you did nothing wrong. About a week ago Laura had a nightmare about being stuck back with Chris and it freaked her out. She didn't want to get hurt again and even though you're not like Chris in any way, she was scared.

She thought it was best to just shut herself off. I could tell she wasn't right at training this week but she wouldn't tell me why until last night. She really misses you Dan. More than you realise, more than even she realised. She's been so deflated."

"I've missed her too," he said, holding back tears as he stared at the coffee table in front of him. "Sarah what do I do? I hate not being around her."

"You care a lot about her, don't you?" She asked, already knowing the answer to her question.

Dan didn't speak straight away as he tried to think of the best way to answer Laura's friend.

"Yeah I do. A lot. Not speaking to her for a week has felt like a life sentence." It was honest. It was all he could ever be.

"Why don't you come over and see her? Last night she was able to admit that she'd really missed you. Maybe talking to you will help her. But you'll need to be very gentle and patient with her, Dan. You seem like a nice guy but listen, I'll have absolutely no qualms in hurting you if you hurt her. Last night Laura was my priority, but trust me, I would have gone in on Chris if she hadn't needed me"

"I couldn't ever hurt her, not intentionally," Dan didn't know what else to say. His world was upside down and inside out.

"Look," she said, "let me send you my address. Come over around 10am. I'll tell Laura you're coming to pick up your jacket and I'll give you two space to talk."

"Only if you're sure." He didn't want to impose but he ached to see Laura, even if only for a moment or two.

"I'm sure. See you in a bit." Sarah hung up the phone leaving Dan sitting in silence, crying into his hands.

I can't put you into words. And my God that frustrates me.
Because you? Oh my God, how I want to write it all down.
Who you are, how I feel about you, why I love you, all of it.
I just want to find or write one fucking poem that could
describe it all. Because damn it what I feel for you
should be written down in permanent ink, it should have
a place of it's own somewhere in this universe;
A place where the words would never, ever cease to exist.

Because neither will my love for you.

~Ccz

Chapter 20

"I'm half a heart without you"

Sarah greeted Dan at the door and quietly let him into her one-bed flat. He looked exhausted and on edge. *Poor guy,* she thought as he walked in.

"She's just in the bedroom. I'll go get her for you, but please be patient with her. She's not great and nothing I'm doing seems to be helping this morning. I can't seem to fix this."

Dan looked her in the eye. "Thank you for letting me see her, Sarah. I'll just see how she is. If she wants me to go, I will. Let's just see how she is when she comes through. There's no pressure or expectation."

Sarah nodded and hoped he'd be true to his word. "Okay."

Leaving him waiting in the kitchen, she went to get her friend.

Dan felt like time slowed down as he waited. Every minute felt like a lifetime. His hands trembled. Standing against the counter he tried to breathe because he knew if he didn't the panic currently held at bay deep inside him would spill over. Laura didn't need to see him like that. Not now. Not after last night. He needed to be strong for her.

~

"Hey." Laura sounded scared as she stood in the doorway to the kitchen, wrapped in an oversized grey hoodie. She looked like an animal just released from captivity, unsure if her new environment was safe or not.

Her eyes were red from crying; signs of drying tears on the sleeves of her hoodie, confirmed it. With the hood down, she'd scraped her hair back into a ponytail to keep it from her face but she'd not bothered with make-up, she didn't see the point. To Dan, she still looked beautiful.

"Hey." Dan mirrored her hello, not wanting to scare her off.

She averted her eyes while crossing the small kitchen, then picked up the kettle and began to fill it with water from the tap. He hadn't asked for a drink but she clearly needed something to do so he didn't stop her or try to talk. He just stood there and watched.

As they waited for the kettle to boil, there was a long drawn-out, awkward silence.

Laura wanted to apologise for everything she felt she'd done wrong and for the person she was. Dan wanted to tell her it would all be okay. But instead, the stalemate went on while the kettle hissed noisily in the corner.

Eventually, Dan had had enough of the awkwardness.

"I missed you. I know I shouldn't, and it's only been a week but it's true. I don't know what we are now Laura but I really miss what we were." He spoke softly.

Laura's tears broke and she walked over to him wrapping her arms around him.

"Dan, I'm so so sorry…" She started to speak, but he stopped her.

"No. I don't want you to be sorry. I want you to be okay." He pulled her close. And breathed her in.

"But…" she tried again.

"No Laura." He held her by the shoulders at arms length and looked deep into her beautiful eyes as he spoke, following her eye line as she tried to avoid looking back.

"All I want is for you to be okay. I desperately want to be your friend and to help you to be happy. But if that's not something you can give yourself to fully then that's fine. I just like being in your atmosphere. I want you to be happy."

Laura bit her lip. "I'm always okay when I'm with you Dan. That's scary to me. I freaked out. I just felt like you'd be better off without me, so I pushed you away."

He gently pulled her back into his arms. "No more pushing away please? My world is bleaker without you. We're in this together okay? You and me. Whatever the future brings." He paused, "Laura, I promise I'll never hurt you like he did. I promise I'll always keep you safe no matter what happens."

"You don't know what he did to me. I hate myself for everything I am and everything he made me. Last week I had a horrible nightmare where he told me again I was ugly and fat, so I panicked and deleted your message without replying. I figured you'd be better off without someone broken like me. Your life feels so perfect and wonderful, and I don't feel like I belong in it. So I pushed you away, which hurt more than I would have thought possible. I'm sorry. I'm truly glad you found me last night."

Tears fell on his top as she spoke. She could feel his body trembling against hers, even though he felt warm.

Dan took a breath and spoke into the top of her head. "I want you in my life, that's why I've allowed you into it. Not everyone gets that chance. I've missed you so much this week, I can't begin to describe it but I promise you I will *never* hurt you like he hurt you. I'd walk through fire to make sure you're ok."

"Thank you," she whispered into his chest, feeling like everything might actually be okay. She could feel herself becoming calmer with every beat of his heart. He felt like he would always be her protector, her lighthouse in the storm.

They stood there for what felt like an hour but the kettle boiling told them it was nowhere near as long. She pulled her head from his warm and welcoming chest and looked up at him.

"Dan? I have something to ask you?"

He lovingly stroked a strand of hair from her face. "Yes?"

"Do you want an instant coffee?" Laura burst out in giggles and for the first time that year the tears that fell were happy ones as she fell back into Dan's arms.

"God, I've missed you," he laughed in reply, "but I have a better idea. Why don't I take you to get a real coffee and then drop you home?"

"Are you sure? I'd really like that, just to spend a bit of time with you," Laura replied.

"If you two are going to be so damned adorable can you please provide advanced warning? I was nearly sick over my breakfast." Sarah stood in the doorway grinning, holding a protein bar. Laura just snuggled into Dan's chest and smiled back at her, with a *look what I've got* expression on her face.

"Thanks for last night, Sarah." Dan's thanks were genuine and heartfelt. Without her, he'd not have Laura back in his life right now.

"Oh shut up dude, it was all you." Sarah smiled at him as if she was taking the piss but her eyes told the truth. She was immensely grateful for everything he had done the night before. Dan nodded back.

"Now if you two have quite finished, I'd really like to get some sleep!"

"Ok let me get my stuff and we'll go." Laura unwrapped herself from Dan and went over to hug her friend. "Thank you for taking care of me last night."

Sarah held her tight and spoke quietly, so only Laura could hear. "I don't think I was the only one taking care of you, babe."

Laura disappeared to get her things along with Dan's jacket, leaving the other two alone together.

"You're good for her, you know. She seems to relax around you." Sarah was still unsure about Dan but her frosty opinion of him was thawing.

"I'm glad one of us is relaxed because I'm a bag of nerves around her."

Sarah put her hand on his arm and smiled, "Just keep doing whatever it is you're doing, it's working." Then she left to catch up on sleep.

~

Five minutes later, Dan was back outside wearing his jacket, with Laura by his side as they walked to the nearby coffee shop. The sun was breaking through the clouds as they walked together.

There he laid looking at me
in a way no one had ever looked
at me. My hands were shaking as
I explained my knotted past. I will not
always be easy to hold onto, for my
heart is scattered with thorns. Some nights
I will be quiet and he won't know how
to pull me from my weeded mind. Some nights
I'll forget what he sees in me and lose my
balance. Some nights I'll trip over my own
feet and apologise for the mess I made. On those
nights the one thing that will drag me out of
my own labyrinth is that look. No one has ever
looked at me quite like that.
~ (j.c.)

Chapter 21

"Father made my history, he fought for what he thought would set us somehow free."

"Daddy? Can I talk to you about something?"

Laura only ever addressed her father as Daddy when she wanted something or when she was in trouble. Dave knew as she opened with it, while hovering in the kitchen doorway, that this conversation would not be good.

"What is it, sweetie?" He replied, folding his paper and putting it on the table in front of him at a tidy right angle to his half-drunk cup of tea.

Laura stayed in the doorway, her eyes downcast, her fingers twirling the silver ring on her right hand.

"I need to tell you something," she began. *This wasn't going to be easy,* she thought. "I've met someone."

The hairs on Dave's neck stood up. "Are you over Chris, Laura? Honestly?"

"No no, Dad. He's just a friend. That's all."

"Oh. So what's the problem? You have lots of friends and you don't always tell me about them. Why is this one different?"

"He's…erm…a bit older than me." She stammered, feeling like she'd just brought the hammer down on her relationship with her father.

Dave only heard two words. *He* and *older*. And both pissed him off in an instant. Laura's father tried to stay calm. He wasn't naturally an angry man but he was known to see red when pushed far enough.

Months before he'd been redlining for ten minutes, driving to the house Laura shared with Chris, to bring her home, his wife's words ringing in his ears, begging him *Dave. Please! Don't kill him!*

As he burst through the door at 4am, he was ready to ignore his wife but he could hear Laura sobbing from the bathroom at the top of the stairs and he knew getting her out was his priority. Chris had just glared at him from the hallway and never moved so much as a muscle.

Now the same anger he felt that night was rising to the surface again but he kept it in check.

"What do you mean he's older?" Dave asked, staring at his daughter in the doorway who still wasn't making eye contact with him.

"He's older than me."

"How much older?" Dave asked, knowing whatever answer she gave would mostly likely be the wrong one.

"He's 38, Daddy." She said quickly.

Dave pinched the bridge of his nose as his eyebrows furrowed. He knew exactly what this friend wanted!

Laura saw the pause as an opportunity to explain but decided a gentler approach was needed now she'd broken the bad news, so quickly moved to sit next to her father at the kitchen table.

"Daddy, you have to understand how good he is for me. We've been chatting on and off for a while. He's such a lovely guy. You'll see, Daddy. He makes me feel better." Laura tried to talk at pace to get it all out before she got cut off.

"How exactly does he do that, Laura?" The insinuation was clear and they both knew it. His words felt like a slap in the face and Laura felt the tears coming.

"Dad! No! Not like that. Honestly, I wouldn't lie to you! We're just friends." As the words left her lips, she knew that wasn't entirely true, and yet she hadn't intended to mislead her dad. She just didn't know how to explain it in a way he would understand, when she didn't fully understand herself.

"So exactly how does he make you feel better then, Laura? This older friend of yours." Dave's hackles were up.

Laura, trembling, put her hand over her father's. It looked so small against his. It always had. She knew right then that his hand would be the one to walk her down the aisle someday and would be the one she held as he slipped into his final sleep. She loved him so much.

"He helps me believe in myself, Dad. He doesn't focus on what's broken in me but on what I am, what I could be. He helps me find my compass in life. I never felt that way with Chris." Just saying his name caused a lump in her throat the size of a small planet. "He genuinely cares about me and I've smiled more around him than I have in months. Daddy, I want you to meet him." In a whisper, she added "it's important to me."

"I need to think about it." Dave replied as he picked his paper and opened it with a flourish. Laura knew he wasn't reading, but she understood the conversation was over.

Rising, she left the kitchen and went into the living room where her mother, Emily was waiting.

"He'll come around honey. Just give him time." She said, pulling her daughter into a brief hug.

Laura stared into nothing, over her mother's shoulder. "I hope so, Mum. I really do."

"If this friend of yours is the good guy you say he is, then your Dad will be okay. He just wants you to be happy."

~

Tues 11th November 3:22pm

Laura: I told him.

Dan: Are you ok?

That was typical Dan, worrying about her first and the

situation second.

Laura: I'm ok. He's not happy. But it was like you said, you're probably the last person he wants me to be friends with right now. He said he'd think about it.

Dan: Well thinking about it is better than a flat out no. Do you want me to back off for a few days and give you space?

Laura: No! Not even a little. Don't go there Dan, please? If you back off, he'll assume the worst things he's thinking about you are true.

Dan: Right, yeah. But Laura, openly defying your dad is a shit place for you to be.

Laura: I know. But for now I'm not defying him. And I really don't want to give up something that's so good for me.

Dan: Ok

Laura: Sorry. I shouldn't have said that.

Dan: If it's how you feel, then you should Laura, you should have said it. I just didn't realise I was so important to you, that was all.

Laura: Of course you are Dan! Are you kidding me? You're quickly becoming one of my closest friends. Our friendship means the world to me. Doesn't it feel that way to you?

Dan: Laura, I'd not give you up for anything. And I mean that.

I'd just rather not have to go into a dual of fates with your dad for your friendship. But if I have to I will. X

First Lesson

The thing to remember about fathers is, they're men.
A girl has to keep it in mind.
They are dragon-seekers, Dant on improbable rescues,
Scratch any father, you find
Someone chock-full of qualms and romantic terrors,
Believing change is a threat -
Like your first shoes with heels on, like your first bicycle
It took months to get.

Walk in strange woods, they warn you about the snakes there.
Climb, and they fear you'll fall.
Books, angular toys or swimming in deep water -
Fathers mistrust them all.
Men are the worriers. It is difficult for them
To learn what they must learn:
How you have a journey to take and very likely,
For a while, will not return.

~ *Phyllis McGinley*

Chapter 22

"And in this world, where nothing else is true, here I am, still tangled up in you"

Laura put her book down in her lap and exhaled. This was the kind of stillness she'd craved since what felt like forever. Sitting on a little pillow in the window frame of Dan's studio, she felt calm and at peace; sheltered in a bubble where the world's troubles couldn't find her.

She looked up and over at the man sitting on the sofa across the room, his salt and pepper hair reflecting the light coming through the window. *I could sit here all day,* she thought, feeling years of tension slowly working its way out of her shoulders.

Watching, she saw him close his laptop and put it on the glass-topped coffee table in front of him. He'd been dealing with emails and client requests all morning while she read. It had been easy and relaxed. Few words had been spoken, but she'd not felt uncomfortable or out of place at all since arriving, on her day off.

Dan ran his fingers through his hair. It was a move she'd

seen him do numerous times now but the slight slump of his shoulders told Laura something wasn't quite right.

"You okay?" She asked gently from her seat in the window, resting her head back on the brickwork behind her.

"Yeah, I'm fine."

Although his answer was short it wasn't dismissive. Putting her book down, she moved to the sofa, drawn by a sense that her sitting next to him was what he needed.

"It's okay if you're not, you know?" She told him gently as she sat next to him.

"Just....I dunno."

"Hey," Laura used a soft voice and let him speak when he was ready. "It's okay. You can tell me anything."

"I got an email from a photographer of the year competition this morning, announcing that they're opening up for submissions from this year's entrants." Dan looked at his hands as he spoke, a sign she knew meant he was uncomfortable.

"That's great, isn't it?"

"Yeah, I guess. I dunno. Just don't feel I've got anything good to submit at the moment."

She wanted to scream at him and tell him that all of his work was beautiful and he was a very special talent. But her heart knew how self-doubt felt and how it sounded. However good his work was, this moment wasn't about what she thought or believed about it. What mattered his own opinion of himself.

"It's like I'm just existing and nothing I'm shooting has that special edge to it. I dunno. Maybe I'm just tired or something. I get a bit like this when I'm tired. Sorry."

He seemed lost. Laura hadn't seen Dan like this before. Maybe the sanctuary he'd built for himself was where this side of him came out and even though it felt like a tough moment for him, she was glad to be here.

He traced his fingers over the back of his phone, where it sat face down on the arm of the sofa. His head was a tangled mess of feelings. Everything in his body seemed to hurt. Deep in his core, there was a sense that he wasn't contributing to the world and it made him ache.

She felt his inner turmoil as she sat and watched him. There was no need to say anything meaningful. Laura just wanted him to not feel alone until his heart let go of his head and he could think straight again.

"If it helps," she said, nudging him slightly with her elbow, "you'll always be my favourite photographer."

A small smile threatened to twitch at the corner of his mouth. All he wanted to do was pull her into him and spend the rest of the day holding her until the thoughts in his head dissipated.

"Sorry," he said again.

"You have nothing to be sorry for Dan. I'm in awe of you every time we meet but that doesn't mean that you're not allowed to feel self-doubt. I just want you to know that in those moments you have a friend who'll listen." She spoke truthfully.

Dan let out a small sigh that seemed to be more of a release of pressure within himself rather than an expression of frustration.

"I just want to feel like I'm enough and that everything I'm working for has meaning. I don't actually care about awards or accolades. I just want to feel like I've made a difference." The smile grew to both corners of his mouth. "Thank you."

Tucking her feet up under herself, she turned towards him slightly. "What are you saying thank you for?" She tried to catch his eye, even though every time he made eye contact, it made her pulse race.

"For not running. I'm not really used to people understanding this."

Smiling, she replied, "oh I don't understand, I think all your work is incredible," she added with a wink, "but I know what self-doubt feels like and how it can hit you out of nowhere. It's easy for people to say" *"oh don't worry you'll be fine"* but I'm acutely aware that the reality of that is a very different thing."

Another sigh. More pressure released.

"I know it's scary to speak about the things your heart doesn't fully comprehend. And while I might not understand why you don't think your work isn't good enough, I do understand how your heart feels."

He pulled his mouth into a contorted funny smile, clearly uncomfortable but more relaxed than moments before. Laura spotted it immediately. She did a similar thing with her nose when she felt awkward.

"Do you know what might help?" She asked, desperately holding a giggle at bay.

"Go on? I'm open to suggestions right now." His smile was more like a proper smile now, rather than a mouth-twitching situation.

"Making a coffee would definitely help you feel better." Laura knew that when she trained, the shitty feelings of self-doubt would recede. Doing something she loved really helped her head.

"Would you like a coffee, Laura?" He laid his blue eyes on her and smiled, cocking one eyebrow at the same time.

"Oh Dan, I'd love one. Thank you so much." The fit of giggles and playful grin that had been waiting for him to react was let loose.

Rising from the sofa with a self-defeating smile, he chuckled and said, "you could have just asked, you know."

"Ah but there's no fun in that," she said as she watched him walk away, simultaneously spinning and sliding down the sofa, to lay horizontally along its length.

"What's up there?" Laura looked up at the stairs near the front door which seemed to lead to a balconied mezzanine above his desk.

Dan turned from the coffee machine. "That's where I sleep."

"Where you sleep? You live here?" She was surprised. It hadn't really occurred to her the last time she was here to consider where he actually lived.

"Yeah. This is my office and my home. I live upstairs. There's a bedroom, kitchen and bathroom up there."

"Huh. I never realised."

Lying on her back on the sofa, looking up at the dark space, she couldn't help but wonder what it was like. But he'd made no effort to show her when she visited, so in her head it felt like a boundary she wasn't meant to cross. A deeper part of his safe place to which he wasn't ready to allow her access.

"When I bought the place a few years ago, it was an empty shell and I'd spent most of my money buying it, so to keep costs down I moved out of the flat I was renting and lived here. That sofa was my bed for a long time."

I'm lying on what was his bed? Shit! She felt like an intruder and started to sit back up.

"Don't worry, it's been cleaned since and it's still one of the comfiest things I've ever owned so don't feel like you can't lie on it." He was slowly and lovingly making her coffee as they talked.

"For a while, this was all I had. Then my friend Martin suggested I add the mezzanine above what is now the storage room, and live up there. So that's what I did. Now this is home. And work."

He gently placed her coffee on the table in front of her as she lifted herself into a sitting position where Dan had been sitting deep in self-doubt moments earlier.

"Doesn't it feel weird? Like just going upstairs after working all day?"

"Yes and no. I guess that's one of the reasons I've taken so much care in making this space my own. That way I want to live and work here."

It was hard for him to explain just how much like home this felt.

"Must be interesting bringing dates back here?" *Laura, you did not just ask that? Jesus!*

For a heartbeat he looked taken aback, as if she'd implied that he was bringing back different women every week.

"Shit Dan, I didn't mean it like that. Sorry." She was crestfallen.

"It's okay. Don't be. To be honest, I haven't really dated for a long time. It just never felt right you know? Maybe I've just not found the right person yet. I'm not really the sleeping around kind, truth be told. I'm waiting on the one. But Martin tells me I'm too picky."

Laura smiled at the fact he didn't sleep around. Not that she cared really, it was his life, but knowing that he wasn't like that comforted her. "Why does he think that? What does she have to be like?"

He looked away and smiled.

"Funny. Smart. Driven by something bigger than herself. Beautiful but not to the point that it defines her. She has to be real. Genuine. Oh and she has to laugh at all my jokes."

Laura looked him dead straight in the eye, and tried not to smile but she couldn't do it and after a few seconds she giggled which made him laugh.

"I'm just looking for the one," he said, as his laughter faded.

"I thought I had the one but I was wrong." She was talking before her brain could engage, but she stayed in the moment. "Now I don't know what I want. All I know is I want to feel loved. Properly."

Sitting in front of him in leggings and hoodie, Dan knew he could love her until the world ended. She ducked her head, averted her gaze and scraped her hair behind her ear as she picked up her coffee.

"So yeah..." The conversation, she felt, had reached a slightly awkward end.

Dan's phone rang on this desk in the corner of the room. As he left to answer it, she relaxed back into the embrace of the sofa and sipped her coffee, staring up into the living space above her and wondered exactly what was beyond the black railing in the dark.

"No, that's okay, let's just go ahead as planned and we can pick up anything that's missed on day two." He was talking to a client, who Laura assumed was anxious about a shoot he was doing. He had a lovely way of bringing calm to the equation when it was needed. She hugged herself slightly and she felt her phone vibrate in her pocket. Pulling it out she saw a message from her dad.

Hey. Look, I'm not saying I'm happy about it just yet but if me meeting this Dan is important to you, then I'd like to meet him. Bring him over on Thursday next week after lunch. He can meet me and your mother and maybe after talking with him I'll feel better about this whole situation. I love you, I just want you to be happy. Dad x

Laura smiled but could feel the nerves flaring in her stomach. Dan ended his call and after returning his phone to it's home on his desk, made his way back to the sofa.

"Dad says he's ready to meet you. Wants to know if you want to come over Thursday afternoon, next week." She said, trying to hold back both her happiness and her nerves.

"Oh." He wasn't disappointed. Just shocked. She knew it would have been a surprise to him but happy curiosity wanted to see what he'd do with this new information.

Smiling, Dan continued, "yeah, I've got a meeting with James but I'll reschedule it. This is more important."

"He doesn't bite you know," she smiled back at him, but her own nerves matched his. *This was really going to happen.* "And he's only seriously injured one of my boyfriends and that was more of an accident…" She let the joke hang for a second as she watched the blood drain from Dan's face.

"You're not funny," he replied, trying to share in the hilarity of her teasing.

I see you

I see your strength and courage,

your hesitation and fears.
I see the way you love others, and
your struggle to love yourself.
I see how hard you work to grow,
and your dedication to heal.
I see your vulnerable humanity,
and your transcendent divinity.
I see you, and
I love what I see

~Scott Stabile

Chapter 23

"When you search the city, for your only friend, it was probably me. "

Laura burst through the line of defenders on their 22, dragging two opposition players with her and could see the try line ahead. All she had to do was hold on and keep driving, but it was hard. Seventy eight minutes of brutal end-to-end rugby on a soaking wet pitch had drained almost every ounce of energy from her powerful legs. She was exhausted.

But they needed this try if they were to have any chance of winning the game. If she could just get the ball over the line and they could kick the conversion, they'd win the match by a single point.

Laura kept pumping her legs. Holding the ball at her chest with her left hand, she pushed down with her right on the defender who was clamped to her leg, and the girl fell away. This sudden loss of additional drag, gave her a burst of speed that brought her within reaching distance of the line.

The last remaining defender adjusted her grip, grabbing hold of the front of Laura's mud stained jersey and she felt her legs going from beneath her. Gritting her teeth and stretching her whole body out with the ball clasped in front of her, she hit the muddy deck and slid forward in the wet. The ball hit the grass still in her hand.

Partly due to exhaustion and partly because the wind had been knocked out of her lungs, she lay there, face down in the wet grass for a second until she heard a whistle blown above her. Before she could register what was happening, she was being hauled up by the jersey and hugged by her fellow teammates. She'd done it. The ball had landed barely over the try line and the ref had blown the score valid.

Sarah pulled her into a hug. "You fucking legend!" She shouted over the noise of the crowd.

As she ran away from Sarah's arms, to allow the kicker to take the conversion that would win the game, Laura spotted Dan in the crowd, clapping and cheering enthusiastically with the other supporters around him. She felt renewed, and it had nothing to do with rugby.

~

"I can't believe you came!" Laura squealed as she ran over to him at the end of the game, rushing into a hug which left him as soaked as she was. "Shit sorry!" But she really didn't care, she was just happy to see him.

Dan chuckled. "Don't be, it's fine." His eyes lit up with happiness. "You were amazing!"

Sweat and raindrops poured down Laura's face but nothing could dampen her spirits. "What can I say I've been in a good place all week and it's showing in my rugby."

They smiled awkwardly at each other for a moment, not wanting to extinguish the little spark that glowed between them in the rain.

"Thank you for being here, Dan. You should have said you were coming though I would've met you before kickoff," she said, blushing. "Although it was a lovely surprise to see you in the crowd." She smiled. He had been making her smile a lot lately and today was no exception

"I was hoping to see the whole game but I got delayed on the motorway coming back from a meeting." He smiled back, never breaking eye contact, not even for a heartbeat.

"Well I'm glad you came," Laura said, holding his gaze, not wanting to look away until she felt someone tugging her by the arm.

"Laura, we need you for a quick TV interview." Laura turned to find the team's media rep Megan, hustling her over to the nearby camera crew.

Calling out to Dan as she was pulled away, she asked, "do you have some time? Or do you need to go?" Her eyes said *please stay*.

"I'm not going anywhere," he called back, restraining himself from adding the word *ever* to his reply.

~

Nearly an hour later, Sarah approached Dan as he leant against the sponsor boards that ringed the now muddy and dark pitch. "Hey Dan. Waiting for Laura?"

"Yeah, I have a little something for her." He jiggled a small white takeaway bag, which only seemed to disperse the smell of glorious spring rolls into the air around him.

"I could reply with so many things right now." Sarah howled and Dan, realising he'd left himself wide open for insinuations, laughed with her. "Fuck me, they smell good though," Sarah added, reaching for the bag with glee.

"Nope!" Dan saw what she was doing and retracted the bag. "If Laura wants to share, that's up to her!" He laughed but guarded his gift like his life depended on it.

"Fine!" Sarah feigned indignation but grinned at him. "She'll be out in a minute. Just takes her a while to dry her hair."

"Figures," Dan replied, his stomach full of excitement as he waited.

There was a comfortable pause between them.

"She played well today, didn't she?" Dan asked, even though he already knew it to be true.

Sarah smiled. It was cute that he'd come to the game that afternoon, just to see Laura play.

"She's been on fire recently. It often happens when a player is in a good place mentally and after recent events, she's been in a great mood," Sarah explained.

"I'm glad," he nodded, smiling a little.

"Thank you, Dan," Sarah said gently.

"Wait what!? What did I do?" Surprised, he had no idea what she meant. But a lifetime's self-doubt, told him he was probably being set up for a fall.

Sarah leant forward on her elbows over the sponsor boards. "You've given her self-confidence."

Dan turned and mirrored Sarah's body position, looking out over the pitch.

"She had that already, Sarah. She just needed to find it again and I'm not sure I did anything to help her with that."

"Bollocks!" She said with affection, "her whole adult life has been spent in Chris's thrall so she didn't know who she really was."

Dan couldn't help but disagree. "It was always in her. She just needed someone to light up the darkness so she could find it for herself. You and her family do that every day."

"Dan, you're a prat. I have no idea why she likes you!" She said, winking at him, "but it's you that lights up her darkness, not us and you have done since we went to Rome." Sarah knew what he'd done, even if he didn't.

He stood awkwardly, unsure what to do. He felt uncomfortable with that level of analysis, his self doubt crept in like a shadow. But she was like a dog with a bone and wasn't letting go of making him feel self conscious.

"She didn't shut up about you in Rome you know, after you two bumped into each other in the airport. Sure she had a few shit moments, but a lot of her time was spent with your name in her mouth. I've been her best friend for a lifetime but sometimes even a friend can't fix every problem or complete every puzzle. You on the other hand, sunshine, seem to fill in the gaps the rest of us can't. And I'm fucked if I know how you do it." Sarah was relishing the opportunity to tease the man next to her, gently barging her shoulder into his with every truth bomb she dropped on his world.

"She doesn't strike me as the sort of person who would need someone like me around. I'm baffled every time she messages me or calls if I'm honest," he replied.

"Never judge a book by its cover, Dan. I thought you'd know that," she joked.

"Sometimes you pick up a beautiful looking book and the inside is even more beautiful," he replied without engaging his brain.

Shit! Did I really just say that?

She knew now. He could see it in her eyes as he looked over at her; that realisation that he'd been keeping hidden, protecting his heart, because he was in love with Laura.

Sarah didn't look at him directly but could see him in her peripheral vision. She didn't want him to know she'd seen through him but she knew full well what she'd witnessed. A chink in the armour this dude wore 24/7. Sarah also knew that she hadn't thawed towards him, she'd positively melted.

"Promise me something, Dan." she said, looking out over the pitch with him.

"Go on," he replied, brimming over with trepidation at what she might ask of him.

"Hold her heart with care. It's probably the most fragile thing you'll ever come across."

Dan knew Sarah knew. Cat out of the bag, toys all over the floor, baby and bath water separated for eternity. There was no point denying it or saying he meant something else entirely. He paused.

"If I have to carry it for a lifetime, I will."

~

A few minutes later, Sarah was gone, climbing into her car and heading away from the ground. Dan's eyes turned towards the player's entrance, a small, nondescript door on the side of the vast stadium wall.

Laura bounced over as soon as she saw him. It was as though

someone had brought a puppy to the game. She couldn't have been more happy if she'd tried.

She stopped short in front of Dan, who was grinning and holding something she couldn't quite make out in his right hand. She tilted her head to the side playfully and stepped up to him, waiting for him to say whatever it was he was clearly dying to say.

"Got you a little something," he said looking down into her bright eyes. He held the bag of spring rolls up and smiled.

Laura, slipping her hand in her pocket to retrieve a small bag of Dan's favourite cola flavoured sweets, said with a returning smile, "swap you?"

Sharing one umbrella
We have to hold each other
Round the waist to keep together
You ask me why I'm smiling -
It's because I'm thinking
I want it to rain forever.

~Vicki Feaver

Chapter 24

"I don't just want to be a memory."

"You okay?" Laura asked as they sat at a table for two at the back of the Rainbow Room cafe, two streets down from her parents' house. They'd decided to meet for lunch ahead of Dan meeting her mum and dad for the first time and she had picked the nearest cafe to where they lived. Sitting together for an hour, they'd talked about her parents and her childhood, while eating sandwiches and drinking coffee from the counter, kindly paid for by Dan.

She felt bad for him, as the long black coffee that he was used to drinking looked like a poor attempt when it was offered to him. She could see he wanted to turn his nose up at it and it would have been cute, rather than offensive if he had done. But, ever the gentleman, he just smiled and accepted it. Their nerves simmered on the surface but being together brought some calm and a chance to take a breath before taking the inevitable plunge.

"Yeah I'm fine, it'll be what it'll be," he said, carefully folding the now empty sandwich packet in half and placing it off to one side neatly. "Maybe a bit of cake will help? Want something?"

"No, it's okay. I probably should watch what I eat really." With anyone else, that reply would have been simple enough, but Dan knew she was making a comment on her shape and size, with feelings of self-consciousness rising to the surface.

Taking her hand, he said, "you're beautiful to me and stuffing your face with cake will *never* change that."

"Go get your cake, smart guy." She said, smiling and waving him off. She knew that no matter what, he'd always accept her.

Minutes later, Dan arrived back at the table with a huge piece of chocolate fudge cake. Two layers of dense, dark sponge cake were held together with a thick layer of gooey fudge fondant and the top was stacked with dark chocolate fudge icing that she just wanted to stick her finger into. She looked at it longingly, wishing she'd asked him to get her a piece.

Seeing her frustration, he smiled and proceeded to delicately dig his fork into the mass of cake, taking a bite. Her eyes tracked the dessert from the plate to his mouth. *Damn it* she thought.

"You know that I don't share cake with just anyone, right? But for you, I might make an exception," he said as he broke off another piece with his fork, making sure this time to get some of the thick icing on top. He held it up between them and looked at her.

"For me?" Laura asked, hoping but not wanting to presume.

He didn't answer verbally but just smiled and pushed the fork forward towards her. Swooning more than she wanted to, Laura leant forward and opened her mouth to take the cake from the fork held in front of her. Her nervous excitement caused her to miss slightly and a cake crumb fell onto her chin. She caught it quickly with a finger, lest it go to waste, and scooped it up into her mouth. *Fuck that's good cake* she thought. Dan just smiled. Seeing her happy always made him happy, no matter what was causing it. Laura's eyes always sparkled a little more when she was happy; it was a heartwarming sight, like seeing a Christmas tree.

"So is this your plan, Dan? Feed my dad cake until he likes you?" She asked playfully.

"Nope. I only have one person that I'd want to feed cake to." Smiling at her, he dug into the cake and offered her another bite, which Laura took without asking. "And anyway, my plan for your dad is to just sit drinking beer, talking about sports and complaining about the general demise of society in the 21st century. That's what men do isn't it?"

She chuckled. If he was nervous he didn't show it. As they shared the rapidly decreasing slab of cake, she wished they could stay like this forever; just happy and content but with added cake.

As Dan placed the cake fork onto the now empty plate, he asked, "so how do you want to do this?"

"What do you mean?" Laura replied, leaning back in her chair, happily full of yummy cakeness.

"Well, do you want to leave my car here and we can walk over to your house? Or do you want me to drive separately and meet you there?" Practicality. That was Dan's staple in stressful situations. "I feel like turning up together in my car might piss him off."

"Erm, no I think it's okay," she said, thinking it through.

"Mum and Dad know we're having lunch here first, so it's not a stretch for them to assume we'd come back together. Especially as I've walked up to meet you. Unless you'd rather not be a gentleman and make me walk home alone." Even though Laura felt nervous, her playful side was getting more comfortable around Dan.

"Fine, looks like we're driving then!" He chuckled as he spoke. "It will be okay, you know," he added. "I'm not a threat to you or your dad. It might just take him some time for him to see it. He's your father, so he wants to protect you and keep you safe. And an older guy like me will always seem like a threat to him and the stability of his family, regardless of the fact that we're only friends. He'll just need some time. I highly doubt he and I will be hugging when I leave later but it'll be okay. You'll see."

"I know. I just want him to like you," Laura said, her nerves building again. "You're really important to me and I just want him to understand that. Mum's happy to go with the flow really, she can tell being friends with you is making me happy, but Dad can be a tough one. He never liked my ex, Chris. But to be fair to Dad, Chris didn't do much to help that situation. You're both really important to me. I just want this to go well."

"It will," he said, placing his hand on hers and smiling to reassure her.

Laura smiled back. She knew it would be alright. Dan just had that way about him. A reassuring way of making everything better with a word or a smile, although she doubted smiles would make the possible situation with her dad okay. But regardless of what happened, she had faith in Dan to do his best to make it right and to do it with a quiet, calming confidence. She hoped one day to be like him, and not a bag of nerves, unable to get her words out right.

"Right gorgeous, we should make a move or we'll be late and that won't be the best start to the afternoon," Dan said, letting go of her hand and rising.

She knew he was calling her gorgeous in reference to her earlier comment about not wanting cake and watching what she ate, but it felt nice. It wasn't out of place or awkward. *Focus on Dad, Laura!* She reminded herself as she stood up.

~

A few minutes later, she was opening the front door and leading Dan into the living room, where her parents waited.

"Mum. Dad. This is Dan."

Stop worrying about
What others will think
Of you when you finally decide
To step out from the shadows.
You've done
The work to awaken yourself
And to remember who you are.
Now it's time to do what
You came here to do.

~maryam hasnaa

Chapter 25

"Cause I'd die if I saw you, I'd die if I didn't see you there...burn up in your atmosphere."

Emily Gray passed her husband his tea, and as was their adorable little way, he thanked her by saying, "I'd give you my last rolo."

Her eyes lit up like they always did, every single time he said it.

"Hey! What about me?" Laura, sitting next to Dan, protested with mock outrage.

He turned his head to her slightly and said softly, "you always get the last spring roll. Promise."

Laura tried to hide her blushes and almost indiscernibly leant into her friend. Her dad put his cup down and stormed out of the living room.

"I'll go," her mother said, sighing. "Sorry Dan."

When they were alone, Laura looked panicked. The thought of her dad being mad at her was awful, such was her love for him.

"Fuck, " she said looking down into her lap.

"It's okay," Dan said, placing his hand on top of hers. "Let me talk to him."

"No it's okay, you don't have to. Mum will sort it." Laura looked at her shoulder as she said it.

"Sometimes, it's better to just confront the issue. I'll talk to him. Trust me it'll be okay," Dan said calmly, as he stood and left.

Laura's fears raged in her as she wondered what the next few moments would hold.

~

A late autumn storm was brewing outside and it was making Dave decidedly irritable. He just couldn't get on with this hanger-on who, despite apparently having a positive effect on his daughter, just seemed to rub the 68 year old up the wrong way without even opening his mouth.

"I don't fucking believe it!" Dave was fuming as he shoved a dirty dish into the sink in front of him and looked out over his pristine garden.

"Dave, calm down. They're just friends. You need to give him a chance."

But Dave didn't care. He knew Dan was going to hurt Laura, eventually. Rage coursed through his veins but he choked it down for her wife's sake.

Storm clouds brewed across the fields behind the house, matching Dave's growing dark mood as he stood by the sink looking out of the kitchen window.

His wife had passed him his drink and stood with him; without even saying thanking her, Dave began trying to process what he should do next.

~

"Can we talk?"

Dave didn't take his eyes from the storm clouds. "I don't have much to say to you, Dan."

"I think we should talk, for Laura's sake." Dan stood still, waiting for Laura's father to accept his presence in the kitchen of the 1930's home. Dave's tea was still hot and he had half a mind to turn and throw it all over the man standing behind him.

"Fine." He nodded to Emily who calmly took her cue to leave, placing her hand reassuringly on Dan's shoulder as she left, giving him a weak smile.

"Look, I know you don't like the idea of me spending as much time with your daughter as I have been doing lately." It wasn't anything more than a statement of fact. Dave remained silent.

"I know there's a multitude of reasons for that Dave. You're concerned about the difference in our ages. You're worried that I just want to have some fun with her and then never see her again. You don't want her to be hurt again. She's been through enough. And being her father, you feel this more strongly than anyone. You want to protect her. Dave. So do I. All I want is for her to be happy. That's it, that's all. Our friendship seems to make her happy and Laura's happiness means everything to me."

Dave thought back to all of the pain that he'd witnessed his daughter go through during the past few months. Anger for her spineless ex, Chris, boiled inside him. He realised he was gripping the counter top in front of him a little too hard.

"Nearly two years ago, Laura was on a photoshoot with me.

That was the first time we met. I captured an image of her," Dan continued. "I couldn't take my eyes off her for the rest of the day after that. I know now that I've been in love with her ever since.

But my only focus is for her to be happy. If I had my way, we'd be together and she'd be happy but that isn't up to me. If our friendship makes Laura happy, then that's how it stays. Friends, My feelings aren't important."

He loves her? Dave was shocked.

"But your relationship with Laura trumps everything else Dave. She's desperate for you to be happy about our friendship and she can tell, I think, that you don't like me. I get it. I know how it seems from the outside. I'm an older guy, she's fragile after a big break-up. For a lot of guys, she'd be easy prey for a fun time. You know that as well as I do."

Dave knew he was right. He'd been on high alert for just this kind of thing ever since that fuck-up Chris had shattered his little girl's heart.

"Dave, I'm not that guy. I promise you that." Dan's voice faltered slightly. "I don't expect you and I to be best friends and go fishing together or whatever, but I'm begging you to see that I only want her to be happy. It's the same thing you want. That's all I want. Just to be in her atmosphere. To see her laugh and smile. We would be better for her, working together rather than apart."

Dave turned and looked into Dan's eyes and could see he was telling the truth. *Fuck*!

"I have no intention of telling Laura how I feel, "Dan said, holding his hands up in defence, "unless she tells me she feels the same way first. I don't want to confuse and upset her. I'm just asking that you try and see that."

Dave took a deep breath. This wasn't the Dan that he'd assumed he'd meet. Somehow he'd convinced himself that he would just be a player and that he wanted nothing but a bit of fun with Laura.

Now as Dave looked at Dan and an eerie stillness settled around them, he realised that he had read the situation wrong. He loved her. And it was a selfless love that he didn't even need Laura to give him in return. Dave and Dan were on the same side. He could see it now.

"And if she loves you back?" Dave couldn't tell for sure, but he suspected his daughter was falling for the man opposite.

"She doesn't. And that's okay. I just want her to be happy." Dan looked away not wanting to meet Dave's gaze.

"Laura, deserves someone better than a guy like me. Someone who can give her the life she wants. The last thing I want to do is drag her into a relationship that doesn't give her what she wants."

Dave watched as Dan struggled for a moment, unable to make eye contact.

He thought back to how broken Laura had been when she'd found out Chris had cheated on her. After a heads up call from Sarah, the first night had been long, as dad and daughter sat talking on the phone. Dave had listened helplessly as his daughter shed tear after tear, before deciding enough was enough and driving to the house she shared with her partner to bring her home. It was 4am, she'd been exhausted and it had taken every ounce of control for Dave not to tear Chris limb from limb.

The pieces had taken a while to fix but Laura was in a much

better place now, not perfect but better. Now Dave felt Dan's pain as much as he'd felt his daughter's all those months ago.

"She deserves to be happy, Dan," Dave said, "It's not about being better or worse. If she's happy with you that's what matters, whether I like it or not."

"I know. But in a few years she might be ready for a family of her own with a man who'll be there for her all the time. I don't know if I can do that. My life isn't conducive to settling down at home with someone. I've created a life for myself that essentially cuts that option off for me, no matter who I love."

Dave gave himself a moment. He knew right now he needed to tread carefully for both Dan's sake and the sake of his daughter sitting in the next room.

"Laura was a mess when she split up with Chris. One minute she was blissfully happy. The next she was in pieces. He shattered her faith in everything and worse than that, he destroyed her belief in herself. She wasn't eating or sleeping. She couldn't see a way out of the pain he'd put her in. She was like a toddler, sat with a broken toy, holding it out pleading, desperate for a grown up to fix it. And I couldn't fix it, Dan. Do you know how heartbreaking that is as a father? But I haven't seen her smile in a long time, not like she has since you've been friends. And whether you realise it or not Dan, I think that's because of you. She's different these days."

Dave remembered how Laura had bounced into the living room a few nights before after a match, in the best mood she'd been in all year.

"I'm sorry for how I reacted a minute ago, Dan. You didn't deserve it." Dave's apology was sincere and from the heart. "I didn't want her to get hurt even though she's been clearly happy that you've come into her life. I could just see how she'd be in a few weeks' time when you'd gotten bored and she'd stop hearing from you."

Dan interrupted before engaging his brain, "I'd never do that!"

"I know." Dave walked around the breakfast counter in between the two men and placed his hand on Dan's shoulder and looked directly at him. "I see that now, and she's happy around you. Happier than she's been in months. What makes you think she doesn't feel the same way as you?"

Pausing to take a long slow breath, Dan spoke softly "I guess I don't know but it terrifies me to find out."

If I still know what love is, it is because of you. I could love you, only you amongst the people. You can't guess what this means. It means the spring in a desert, the flowering tree in a wilderness,

~Hermann Hesse

Chapter 26

"I'm starting with the man in the mirror"

As the weeks passed, Dan and Laura spent more time together; the photographer quickly became one of her closest friends.

While Dave hadn't welcomed him as a member of the family quite yet, he did his best to accept Dan in his daughter's life. He seemed to bring out the best in her.

Dan, for his part, was careful to not flaunt their friendship in front of her parents, even at times attempting to calm her enthusiasm.

"I know, but maybe your parents could use a little break from seeing my face there all the time. It's their home, not mine," he'd said one morning when Laura had suggested they have a movie day round there on her day off.

Dave and Emily had watched how the pair had been around each other. For the first time in months, their daughter seemed content. Her growing confidence was apparent.

Dan was a gentleman, a true friend to her and offered her his unwavering support. While Dave knew the truth, he could see that the more often he saw them together, that Dan's true intentions were simply to make his daughter happy.

A defining moment had come when he'd overheard Laura sharing her fears in a moment of doubt about putting herself up for selection for the England team, her childhood dream. Standing in the kitchen doorway sipping a glass of water, Dave had heard Dan in the hallway with his daughter reminding her that she was in control of her life.

"You got this Laura. You don't need to live the life you used to have with him, you're a strong, confident woman now and I'll be right behind you cheering you on".

He could hear the smile in his daughter's voice when she replied, "go big or go home, right?"

Dave couldn't help but warm to the guy. He was a good man who would go to the ends of the earth to make sure Laura would live the best version possible of her life. He knew he had an ally not an enemy in him.

Ahead of two nights away with his wife, Dave had even given Dan his number in case of emergencies or in case he needed anything. He knew Laura didn't like being in the house alone, she never had, and he trusted Dan to keep an eye out for her should she need it. He was a good guy and the trust Dave had in him was growing.

Sometimes it just
takes someone loving you
the right way to remind you

that you've always been
worth loving.

~Dane Thomas

Chapter 27

"When I'm feeling blue, all I have to do, is take a look at you"

"Thank you for coming! You're my hero." Laura said, opening the door to Dan, who was standing on the front step.

He smiled a half smile just like he always did when he saw her. "Less of a knight in shining armour and more of a twat in tatty tinfoil," he joked as she let him in.

"What would I do without you?" She smiled back.

He could hear the banging from the noisy boiler upstairs.

"What did your dad say?" He asked, trying to make it seem like he knew what he was talking about. He didn't.

"Dad says it just needs turning off and on again." He gave her a quizzical look. "Hey, I know okay! But I can't figure out how to turn it off. I'm genuinely worried it's going to explode and take half of the street with it! You wouldn't want me to be blown up? Would you, Dan?" She fluttered her eyelashes at him.

"For the love of God!" He joked. "Show me."

They headed up the stairs and Laura showed him the cupboard in the hall, where the boiler banged noisily, positively fidgeting behind the door.

"It's in here," she said, backing away slightly.

Opening the door, Dan sensed her distress. "Hey. It's okay. I'll sort it." *Fuck knows how* he thought.

Flicking on the torch on his mobile phone, he peered around inside the cupboard. It really did feel like this thing was going to explode any second. Dan felt like he was a bomb disposal expert. *Stop being a prat,* he told himself.

After a few heart-in-mouth seconds, he located the override power switch, tucked away at the back of the cupboard, hidden in the shadow of the boiler. Hitting the switch, the banging stopped immediately and he heard Laura taking a deep breath as the crisis had been averted.

"My hero." She mocked him again but he knew it was affectionate. "Dad said to switch it back on and that should just sort it. Can you do that for me too? Please?"

He stood up and faced her. "I did it when you were deriding my shining suit of armour." They both laughed. "It seems okay now," he added.

She smiled at him but he could tell she was still reticent about it.

"When are they coming back?" He asked her.

"Tomorrow," she replied quietly, a tinge of anxiety in her voice. "They have another night in the hotel and then they'll drive back after lunch."

"You gonna be okay?" He asked even though he knew he wouldn't get a completely truthful answer.

"Mhmmm," she murmured, looking away.

He took her smaller hand in his. She turned back to look at him, scrunching up her nose awkwardly. "Go grab some overnight things in a bag. You're staying with me tonight. I don't want you to be alone. I'll call your parents and let them know. "

"Dan, no," she started to say but he stopped her.

"You've seen my massive sofa right? I've slept on that thing so much, it's like a second bed. You'll have my bed which is on its own separate floor. You'll have complete privacy."

Admitting defeat and knowing it was for the best, she said, "thank you. You really are my hero." She gave him a brief hug before exiting the hall to her bedroom.

~

"Yeah okay, Dan, she's never liked being alone in the house at night. Thank you. We'll be back home tomorrow afternoon. Call me if you need anything." Dave said, reassured that his baby girl was being looked after in his absence.

"No worries. Enjoy your last night and say hi to Emily from me."

~

Hanging up the phone to her dad, Dan waited at the top of the stairs for Laura while she quickly packed. He'd made sure to have the call on speaker phone with Dave, so she could overhear the whole thing. The last thing he wanted was for Laura or indeed her dad, to feel anxious about her sleeping at his place.

Her bedroom door opened slightly and she snuck out, trying to hide what lay behind the glossed white wooden door. For a split second, he caught a glimpse of medals hung on the wall above a dresser with stickers on the drawers. She closed the door quickly.

"Please don't look," she cringed. "It's so embarrassing."

"Laura," he said, as they stood at the top of the stairs. "You are your past, good and bad and I will never judge any of it. I promise."

Taking the bag from her, he turned and made his way down the stairs, with the girl following in step.

~

Wine snorted from her nose, as Laura tried to fight off the giggles. Dan laughed, as much at his story as at her.

"And that's the truth. I stood there drenched from head to toe."

It took a few minutes for her to breathe properly again and for her eyes to stop watering.

They'd been trading stories all evening while sitting on Dan's sofa, working their way through a Chinese takeaway and sharing a bottle of red wine. .

She put her wine glass down and flicked the bag of spring rolls next to it, in the hope there was one left. There wasn't. Her eyes drifted to the picture book that she'd seen every time she'd visited. Like the half bottle of whiskey, it was a constant that resided on his coffee table.

"Why that book?" She asked. "I feel as though it's an intentional choice." Everything was intentional with Dan, she knew this very well by now but she was still curious.

"It was my mum's. I remember lovingly flicking through those pages as a kid, sitting on the living room floor at home, looking at all the black and white pictures inside. I guess I've been chasing images like that my whole life." He paused, as if he was lost in a memory. "I lost both my parents in the space of ten days a few years ago. Mum, after a long battle with cancer. Dad the following week from a heart attack. Well, that's what the doctors said. I think he died from a broken heart; that's how much they loved each other." He stopped for a moment, trying to find the words.

Before he could start talking again, Laura wrapped her arms around his neck and pulled him close. It wasn't so much that he needed it, but the only thing she wanted was to hold him.

"I'm okay. I worked through it a long time ago." He said into her shoulder. As she let go slowly, but stayed close, he continued.

"I didn't want much of theirs, when I went through all their stuff to sell the house. But that book was important to me for lots of reasons, so along with my first ever camera and Dad's wedding ring, it got brought here and it has stayed on my coffee table ever since."

"Do you miss them? Sorry, stupid question!" She asked, hating herself for asking without thinking.

"I do, yeah. Theirs was the greatest love story ever told in my eyes. Every reference I have to real love comes from them. They were and always will be, my model for what love should look like. I want that for myself one day." He looked longingly into his wine glass.

"I'm sorry," she said quietly.

"Don't be," he replied, lifting his eyes to her. "You have nothing to be sorry for. I wanted you to know. I'm made up of my past. To know me, means you need to know the things that have made me who I am. And I want you to know me, Laura."

She thought about what he'd said for a moment. There were

days when her parents drove her nuts but she could never imagine not having them in her life. He was alone in the world and she felt for him deeply. A desire to be open and vulnerable with him swelled in her briefly.

"I had a dream that my life would be different to this hell I'm living," she said. "It wasn't meant to be like this. Mum and Dad have been amazing these past few months but I feel like I've been dragged back into a life I thought I'd outgrown. It's been really hard. But now that I hear about your parents, I feel like I ought to appreciate how fortunate I am."

She stopped and went quiet.

"You're allowed to feel upset and fucked off,Laura. You've been through hell and had to take steps to get out of that. I get that it feels like you've gone backwards, but often in life you end up on the wrong road without realising it and the only way forward is to go back and find another way. You've found another way now." He spoke softly, with a calmness to his voice that felt like a warm hug.

"Thank you Dan. For everything. I'm not sure I could have survived this last year without you."

He put his hand on top of hers where it rested on her knee. She felt a spark flick between them. In an instant it was gone.

~

Laura yawned a little. It was getting late and she was tired. Even though he could have sat talking to her till the sun rose, hours later, Dan knew that he had to let her sleep.

"Come on you. Bedtime." He said, smiling.

"No, I'm okay. Promise. Let's keep talking for a bit longer."

"Nope. You're training tomorrow morning, and as much

as I want to talk the night away, you need some sleep." He replied, fighting every urge in him to let her stay with him on his black sofa.

"Alright, Dad." She winked as she said it but Laura was secretly relieved. She was knackered and was looking forward to closing her eyes.

~

Taking her bag from where she'd left it by the front door, he led her up the single flight of stairs. After wondering what his living space looked like when it had been previously hidden in the dark from her, she feasted her eyes on the large, open-plan balcony area that sat partially above his workspace and storage area. It was spacious and mirrored the methodical organisation of his studio below. Pushing a button on the wall at the top of stairs, the room lit up with mood lighting from under the bed, under shelves and around the small kitchen area. As Laura looked through tired eyes, it all seemed to twinkle.

"Dan, it's beautiful!" She exclaimed.

"Always with the tone of surprise." It was his turn to wink and gently tease her. "It's just a place to sleep." He turned to smile at her. "So it's pretty self explanatory; this is my bed, the kitchen is over there. The fridge has fresh water in the door, so help yourself if you need any. The bathroom is through that door over there," he pointed to the back corner of the room, next to the kitchen area. "There's a wireless charger on the nightstand there for your phone….what else? Oh. Yeah, the blinds."

Laura looked confused. The space, while a delight for the

eyes, had no windows. It was just the mezzanine upper section of the space below, which had windows. So why would she need to know about the blinds?

She watched as Dan walked over to what she assumed was his side of the bed. Picking up a small black remote, he pointed it up to the high ceiling and pressed a button. A whirring took her attention above.

There, sunk into the roof, was a square no bigger than a small side table. As she watched she realised what she was looking at. It was a skylight, and a blind was drawing back on it, controlled by Dan's remote. A shaft of moonlight slid through the gap above her and bathed the room in a soft white glow.

Is he making this shit up? She thought to herself.

"It's nice when the moon is out. But it's probably worth shutting it before you fall asleep or you'll be woken at sunrise. It's up to you though. The remote stays here on my nightstand," he said, placing it carefully back in its place by the bed. As he did, she noticed that next to it was an old framed picture of a couple on their wedding day. A single silver ring sat in front of the matching silver frame. *His parents,* she thought. Her heart ached a little for him. *His model of true love* he'd told her. She could see why he'd want to keep them close.

"Thank you Dan. I really appreciate this," she said.

"You're welcome. I'll be downstairs if you need anything. Shout me in the morning and I'll get the coffee on the go." With that he smiled, walked past her and made his way down the stairs.

Laura picked up her bag that he'd had left at the foot of the bed, and went to get out her clothes for sleep. But something wasn't right. Her training kit was there but her PJs weren't. Panicking, she searched the bag three times. She thought back to packing the bag in her room earlier in the afternoon. She hadn't picked them up. She'd put them next to her bag to pack them but she'd never put them in.

"No no no no no!" Laura said aloud.

Dan came back up the stairs moments later. "What's wrong? You okay?"

She felt embarrassed and awkward. "I forgot my PJs," she said sadly. "I thought I'd packed them but I must've left them on my bed."

"Ah," Dan replied, thinking. "Well, okay." He walked calmly over to his dresser on the right hand wall and pulled open the second drawer down. "So this is my t-shirt drawer," he said, "have a look through and see if there's anything you think you'd feel comfortable sleeping in. If not, don't worry, we can nip you home to pick your PJs up. It's your call." He left her to choose, leaving via the stairs for the second time in as many minutes.

Laura sighed and made her way over to the drawer, thinking about how her body was bigger than his and most likely nothing he had would fit over her curves. She looked through the array of t-shirts on offer, unsurprised to see a selection in every shade of black or grey imaginable, all neatly folded and stacked. *So very Dan.* Choosing one, she pulled it out carefully. It was clean but still smelt of him. Unfolding it and holding it against her body, she quickly decided it would be too snug. Although she might not be on show while asleep and Dan would obviously be a gentleman, she didn't want that awkward feeling in something that hugged every curve and fold she had. She put it back.

As she was about to give up and ask him to take her home so she could retrieve her own PJs which she'd clearly left neatly folded back on her bed, she spotted a flash of unfamiliar colour amongst the sea of black in the drawer. Curious, she took it out to find that it was a navy blue, NFL jersey from what she assumed was his favourite team. It had a giant white number 6 on the front. Her spirits rose. It looked much bigger than the rest. Quickly holding it next to her body, she realised she had a winner and went to the bathroom to change.

As she slipped out of her clothes, she looked around. It wasn't big. No bigger than the size of a hotel room bathroom really, but it was beautiful. A white sink set in a white counter which housed a collection of Dan's toiletries; deodorant, aftershave and a toothbrush, *he's quite the minimalist* she mused. To her right there was a large shower with a full length glass panel, separating it from the rest of the room. Inside, she noticed it had a huge shower head which must be like standing in a rain shower. Her mind conjured up images of the shower full of steam and Dan behind the glass. She shook the thought away as quickly as it appeared.

Pulling the American Football jersey over her head, she knew it would be fine for the night. It felt spacious enough, if a little short on the leg. *As long as I don't try and touch my toes it'll be okay*. The jersey's heavy fabric felt expensive and comforting; he clearly hadn't just bought a cheap fake online.

~

Climbing into Dan's bed minutes later, Laura groaned inwardly. *God, this bed is amazing,* she thought. In contrast to all the black in his life, his bedsheets were white and topped with a big fluffy duvet and soft luxurious pillows. It felt like she was in heaven. The bed smelt like Dan too. She melted into its comfort and smiled contentedly. Looking up she saw the glowing moonlight above her head and let out a relaxed breath; he hadn't been exaggerating about the skylight. The bed was so soft and warm, it was like lying on a cloud. It left her feeling safe and almost as if he was surrounding her.

Reaching for her phone; she quickly messaged him, lying on the sofa a floor below, to thank him for the t-shirt and to say good night, before sleep took her.

~

Dan sat, perched on his sofa and gulped down a glass of water. It was 5:02am and still dark outside, The glow of street lights three floors below was visible through the gaps in the blinds. He thought back to a few minutes before when he'd been dreaming about her as he lay fast asleep.

Laura had crawled up his bed to him and kissed him deeply, a playful look in her eyes, nibbling on his lip. His hands had started on the soft skin of her thighs, just above the knees, and slid casually up and over her bottom. She'd purred as he'd eased them gently over her hips and then slowly up her back, applying a gentle pressure with his fingertips as he did so, making her moan into his mouth. He could feel her naked body against his own as they got tangled in the sheets together. Smiling at him she'd guided herself...

And then he'd woken up. She'd felt so real.

He cursed his bad luck for waking up just when it was getting good. But as he thought about it, he felt ashamed and guilt washed over him for thinking about her like that as she slept soundly above him. It wasn't right. They were only friends and his lust for her, even if only in a dream, felt unfair.

~

Sun sprinkled rays through the skylight above the bed and Laura covered her eyes as she remembered she was meant to close the blinds before falling asleep. Realising where she was, she smiled at the comfort of her immediate surroundings. She had one pillow beneath her head and another cuddled into her arms and she wondered, for a moment, who or what she'd been dreaming about. A smile was taking over her whole body. She swung her legs out of the bed and grabbed a pair of socks from her bag at the side of the nightstand to keep her feet warm on the wooden floor. Padding across to the balcony wearing only Dan's loose navy NFL jersey and her recently added socks she hoped he was awake. Leaning on the rail, she looked down. She could see the sofa - but it was empty; a plain white duvet folded neatly on one end. Where was he?

"Dan?" she called softly. "Hey."

"Good morning." His warm deep voice felt exactly like the sunlight hitting her face. She heard him before she saw him and he walked out from where his desk sat under the lip of the balcony, with his pen in hand. *He's been journalling?* She wondered.

"Hey." She smiled down at him, conscious of how she was dressed, her bare legs only partially hidden by the railing she was now leaning on. She felt exposed and would have withdrawn but she realised that actually, she didn't feel threatened. It was curious.

"How'd you sleep? Would you like a coffee bringing up?" He asked, smiling back.

She nodded enthusiastically and retreated to the warmth of the bed while she waited.

Dan flicked on the small gooseneck kettle next to his coffee machine and dropped a filter into his V60 pour over brewer. As he made them each a cup of coffee, he tried to focus on the task in front of him but all he could think about was how she'd slept in his bed while wearing his favourite jersey. She looked mind-blowingly sexy in it, casually leaning over his balcony looking down at him, with her hair loose and messy. He longed for a life where that vision was what greeted him every day.

"One morning coffee," he said, cresting the top of the stairs, finding her smiling to herself tangled up in his bedsheets in front of him. He paused just to take it all in.

"Dan, just to make you aware," she said curling herself up in his big duvet and looking like butter wouldn't melt, "that this is my bed now. I'm never leaving it. Feel free to move your stuff downstairs and sleep on the sofa. I'm staying forever."

Smiling, he placed her mug of coffee on the nightstand next to her. Laura's pulse quickened, not because she was excited but because she suddenly realised that he might sit on the bed with her while she was wearing hardly anything. But, after placing the mug down, Dan gently retreated to the railing with his coffee. He was giving her space, while still wanting to stay where he could see her. She looked at him through the covers.

"Not sorry," she smirked.

Dan sipped his coffee and smiled back. "Big words for a little girl," he replied without thinking. Then quickly added. "You have training in a few hours. You'll get out of that bed yourself before I have to make you." He winked.

Sitting up to drink her coffee, Laura kept her body hidden with the duvet. She looked at him. Leaning against the railing, he stood in a dark t-shirt and grey sweatpants. His hair had a fluffy bed-head quality that was cuter than she needed to see at that time of the morning. She raked her eyes from his unusually messy hair to his bare feet on the hardwood floor. She was only really used to seeing him in jeans and while the sweatpants looked different, it wasn't jarring. Her glance slid over his flat stomach and lower, blushing slightly when she realised she was openly looking at how the grey fabric clung to his form. *Why can't he just look like a troll in the morning* she thought as she realised she could get used to that sight.

"So how did my bed treat you? Did you get much sleep?" He asked, peering over the top of his coffee cup.

"Your bed? Dan, you really need to accept that ownership of the bed is now mine," Laura chuckled, "but yes I slept like a baby thank you. How is this bed so comfortable?"

Smiling, he said, "A few years ago, I went through a stage of struggling to sleep so I invested in the best mattress and pillows I could find that would suit me. What you're currently tangled up in, is as perfect a sleep experience as I've been able to create to date."

"Well whatever you did, it's bloody glorious!" She said slipping down into its comfort a little to enjoy her hot coffee.

"Breakfast?" He asked, motioning to the adjacent kitchen area.

"Keep saying all the right things Dan..." She giggled.

"Ha" He laughed out loud as he walked across the room. "Erm, so I have some bacon in, I think? I can make toast. I don't think I have any cereal, sorry."

"If you feed me bacon, I'll be yours forever," she joked, then instantly regretted it, falling silent.

"Bacon it is then."

~

An hour later, Laura was full of coffee and bacon rolls as Dan showered upstairs. She was filled with a sense of gratitude. The day before, she had been looking down the barrel of a night alone with only a noisy boiler and her intrusive thoughts for company. But he had saved her from that. He always made sure she was okay. He was always there ready to catch her whenever she stumbled. No matter the circumstances, he was always right there whenever she needed him. She smiled into her second cup of coffee.

As her mind wandered to the week ahead, Laura thought about the annual rugby Christmas dinner dance held in the centre of town every year. It was due to be held in the Bailey Room, the ballroom at the prestigious Marriot Hotel on Friday night. She'd already picked her dress out online and was about to buy it on her phone that morning, when she heard Dan coming down the stairs, strapping his watch to his wrist.

"Hey, what do you think of this?" She asked, pulling up a picture and turning her phone, so that he could see the flowing red dress on the screen.

"Yeah, it's really nice. What's it for?"

"Oh it's for that dinner dance thing that happens every year at Christmas. Do you like it? I'm thinking of wearing it." She really didn't know what he'd think of the dress, as he only really ever saw her in comfy clothes.

"Like it?" Dan replied, slightly shocked. "You'll look amazing in it."

"Ah I don't know about that. I just want to look nice, you know?" Her self-confidence ebbed away slightly and she began to fill with nerves.

Noticing her retreating into herself slightly, he pulled her up by the hand and stood her in front of him. Placing his hands on her hips, he looked longingly into her eyes, seemingly trying to look into her soul.

"Laura, you have to understand that to me, you are always and will always be the most beautiful woman in any room. You wouldn't look nice in that dress, you'd look stunning." His eyes never left hers as he spoke.

Laura held his gaze and looked back. His gentle hold on her hips was making her belly tense and she felt fidgety in a way no man had made her feel before. "Do you mean that? She asked tentatively.

Dan smiled, "with all my heart." He turned her towards the window and she could see their reflection staring back with him behind her. "Look," he said.

She followed his instruction. Usually hating her reflection, Laura forced herself to look and felt a level of calm as she saw him standing with her looking back, an easy smile resting on his lips.

"Can you see a little of what I see? A beautiful woman, with her whole life ahead of her." His hands stayed on her hips in a gesture that felt like he was trying to steady her and keep her fleeing from herself. He wanted her to see herself through his eyes.

As Laura looked, she felt something shift in her. Looking back from the reflection, she didn't see a broken girl any more or one to be kept in check. What she saw smiling back wearing dark leggings and a grey form hugging t-shirt, was a beautiful woman, with curves that didn't repulse her but that she knew she could work to catch the eye of someone special. Her blonde hair piled loosely on her shoulders, and falling onto her chest; it looked really good when she left it down she realised. And her smile, something she usually hated, seemed to portray an inner power that was starting to build in her as her confidence had slowly grown without her having really noticed.

Dan didn't need an answer to know she'd seen it. He smiled and said, "see? That's what I see, every day. I think you'll look wonderful in that red dress."

She turned and hugged him. She didn't know what to say, as every version of thank you in her head seemed to leave her wanting to say more, so she just let him hold her as she smiled. She'd seen it, what he saw, for the first time.

I am pieces of all the places I have
been, and the people I have loved. I've
been stitched together by song lyrics,
book quotes, adventure, late night
conversations, moonlight,
and the smell of
coffee.

~Brooke Hampton

"Dan and Sarah"

Wednesday 8th: 8:02pm

Sarah: Dan. Help! Our photographer just dropped out for the annual dinner dance on Friday night!! Is there any way you could do it? Please? We're desperate.

Dan: Hey. Yeah of course. Just drop me some details and I'll make sure to be there for you. Don't worry I got you. What time do you need me?

Chapter 28

"If I can't have you right now, I'll wait dear. All we need is just a little patience."

Sitting on his sofa, Dan dropped a portable flash into his black Think Tank camera case, looked over to his left and stared out of the window. He knew he probably wouldn't need the light for that night's event but he felt so indecisive that he couldn't really settle on anything. He was distracted. As he looked out over the grey, wintery skyline, his mind flashed back to the last time he'd been invited to the annual rugby dinner dance.

~

Laura sat on the end of the bed, staring at the dress, hidden in its protective bag hanging on the side of Sarah's wardrobe. *What a difference two years makes,* she thought. Then, she'd gone to the annual dinner with Chris and she'd felt out of place the whole evening, even though she'd done her job well of putting a brave face on throughout. Now she knew, as she pictured her outfit for the night, that she wouldn't want to be anywhere else and any smiles that would be on show, would be genuine.

~

Leaving his kit bag open and half packed on the coffee table, Dan moved to the windowsill and sat where Laura had taken to sitting and reading when she visited. It felt more like home when Laura was there. Looking through the window at the street below, his mind took him back to two years before.

A client, who happened to be on the board of directors for one of the clubs in attendance, had invited him as their guest to the annual dinner dance. Dan saw the evening as a good chance to do some networking and maybe meet some potential new clients. He liked to refer to this part of the job as shaking hands and kissing babies. The whole networking thing made him feel like a politician canvassing for votes. He hated it. But it had never occurred to him that she'd be there.

Noticing her across the room, she'd been standing with a bearded man. That evening Laura had worn simple black trousers and a pink top with three quarter length sleeves and a high neck. She looked pretty. She always did whenever he saw her. But he could see in the way she held herself, that she didn't want to be there. The man with her, smiled broadly but Dan knew it was a smile that merely sat on the surface. It was only for show. Any casual observer would see a happy couple out for an evening. But he remembered, as he watched cars driving past below his window, how even then he had the sense she wasn't happy. But at the time, with what, he hadn't known.

~

Laura could still feel how Chris's fingers had dug into her left arm, as he'd led her around the ballroom while they talked to people. This wasn't uncommon for her fiancé. To him, she was a prize to be shown off whenever he wanted. But a prize that wasn't allowed to shine too brightly. He liked her to be at his side when they went out anywhere and would often hold her just above the elbow, guiding her. Sometimes those fingers would dig in a little deeper than usual. The thought made her shudder briefly.

She thought back to all the times in the last year, when Dan had gently held her hand whenever he'd felt like she needed it. Those moments were never about control. He made her feel safe, protected and cared for. She sighed happily.

~

Remembering how the evening had seemed to drag on, Dan recalled being approached by Sarah for the first time. She'd introduced herself and enquired about the potential for getting some match day photos in the new year, as the team's usual photographer would be away for a few weeks. They'd chatted a little about what he could do for them, reminisced about the photoshoot a few months prior and they'd ended the conversation by exchanging numbers; Sarah promising to call after the Christmas break to set something up. She seemed nice enough and Dan had felt positive that he had made a new business contact.

~

Looking down at her hands as she sat on the bed, Laura could vividly recall how she'd been on edge all night, two years ago, while her fiancé had laughed and joked with their friends. He had left her sitting alone at their table, pushing a half-finished dessert away having lost her appetite. She remembered how she'd seen Dan across the ballroom but hadn't really thought much of it at the time. *How different could my life have been?* She wondered as she thought about him.

Over the last few months, he'd become her rock. She'd felt her trust in him growing with every moment they spent together, her previous fears gone. It wasn't that he'd torn her defences down like an invading army; more that he'd sat patiently and waited for her to dismantle them herself. He'd become the space in-between the spaces of her life.

She knew he wasn't perfect. He could be irritable when things were troubling him and he suffered a lot from feelings of self doubt. But she'd never been scared by that, it just made her feel more deeply for him.

~

Dan moved back to his partly packed case and away from Laura's seat by the window. He remembered how two years prior, he'd seen her sitting by herself at one point. She'd looked alone. Truly alone. He vowed to himself that if he saw her looking like that tonight, even though he was working, he'd go to her. He never wanted her to feel alone again.

He thought back to all the times they'd spent together. How much she'd grown and changed over the past few weeks. She seemed so much stronger and more self-assured now. It made her yet more attractive to him. He hoped that he'd helped to make a difference in her life but simultaneously was content to just have been around her and made no difference at all.

~

She carefully lifted the dress down from the wardrobe and carried it to Sarah, who was sitting in her living room.

"Sarah? You want to see my dress for tonight?

Her friend put her phone down, stood up and looked expectantly as Laura unzipped the bag that hid her plan for the evening.

"Holy cow!" Sarah was so shocked she took a step back. "I thought you were getting that red one?"

Chapter 29

"Take these broken wings and learn to fly"

Laura just chuckled. "It's pretty isn't it? I was gonna go for the red one but, well I felt like wearing something a bit different."

"Pretty?" Her friend replied in shock. "It's not pretty, it's bloody gorgeous! Are you kidding me? And you just *felt like* wearing something different Laura! Dan's coming now and you want to blow his mind. Just be honest."

Laura blushed. For the first time in a long time she felt confident and was excited to get ready for the annual dinner dance, held by the great and the good of the rugby world. After finding out that Dan was going to be there a few days earlier, trying on her new choice of outfit for the evening, she knew it was the one. She felt amazing in it.

"Maybe I do, yeah."

Her friend chuckled. "Right let's do this then, our hair appointment is in half an hour. Put your seduction outfit back in the bedroom and let's get Cinderella ready for the ball." Sarah checked her watch as she hustled Laura to get a move on. Once a leader, always a leader.

~

Sitting in front of the barber's mirror, Dan felt a familiar anxiety building inside him. His skin tingled and a pain was building between his eyes that threatened to darken his vision. *It's just nerves* he told himself.

He wasn't worried about the booking tonight. Even though it was a short notice thing, it wasn't out of his wheelhouse. He just didn't intentionally do this kind of work through choice if he could help it. There was nothing to be nervous about with his camera in his hand.

But Laura would be there. And he wanted to look his best. *But was this too much effort? He didn't want to stand out.* His anxiety flickered. *What if he was going to too much trouble? What if she thought he was trying too hard?*

The haircut looked good. He always trusted Adam, his barber, to do a good job. But his mind wandered back to the freshly pressed black suit hanging from the wardrobe door in his bedroom. *Was it too much?* It felt too late now to change his mind. The dull ache between his eyes persisted.

~

Sarah looked over at her friend in the next seat. *Those soft curls really accentuate Laura's face,* she thought. The change in her friend over the last week or so had been remarkable and she knew full well what the cause was. She smiled.

Whether Dan knew it or not, he'd helped Laura realise she was a beautiful, confident woman and sitting next to her, Sarah could see the glow radiate from her. *If he knows what he's done and this was intentional, that man is a God,* she thought.

Laura smiled at the hairstylist behind her who adjusted her fresh curls to let them sit delicately on her shoulders. Looking at herself in the mirror, she knew she looked really good even though she wasn't even in her outfit yet.

~

He could never do ties and it took four attempts for Dan to get the simple black tie to sit at the right length. The collar of his white shirt sat a little too tight around his neck but leaving the top button undone with the knot of his tie in place, he hoped it would provide some breathing space.

Donning his suit jacket, Dan glanced at himself in the mirror. He looked sharp and stylish without overdoing it. Would she look at him as a friend tonight? Or would she see him as the man who loved her?

~

Sarah eyed Laura smoothing her black lace basque and straightening the seams of her stockings. "You're so hot babe!"

Laura laughed, "I know!"

"Get you!"

Laura shrugged "I have eyes and mirrors…" They both laughed.

Stepping into her sparkly dress, Laura let out a slow breath as she looked at herself in the full length mirror. There was nothing else to add. Her makeup was done. Her hair was finished with a simple but beautiful silver clasp which sparkled to the left side of her face. Sarah had kindly lent her a stunning opal necklace which matched her gown perfectly. Laura gently turned the silver ring on her finger as the nerves threatened to invade her confidence.

No. I got this, she told herself. She smiled. She looked and felt incredible.

Gone was the girl who months before had stood in front of the mirror in a hotel room in Rome, hating her body and ashamed of who she was. Now looking at the reflection before her, she could see she had been set free and Laura was starting to understand who had breathed life into her. She smiled at herself in the mirror. Tonight was about unfurling her wings and learning to fly.

~

Zipping up his black flight case, Dan took a last drink of water from the glass on the counter in his kitchen and got set to leave. This was either going to be a long night of painful torture or the best night of his life. And right now it was on a knife edge, which way it would all go. "Right. Go big or go home," he said aloud as he turned the handle on the door to his apartment and left into the night.

~

Laura sat calmly in the back of the Uber with Sarah. Her usual butterflies were away somewhere else this evening; she felt in control. The smile on her face, for once, didn't feel out of place.

"What?" Sarah asked, studying her friend beside her.

"Nothing." Laura's smile didn't fade.

"Nothing, my arse! Why the Cheshire Cat grin?" Her friend wasn't taking *nothing* for an answer tonight.

Laura bit her bottom lip, "I'm just thinking about walking in and seeing Dan standing there, that's all."

Sarah laughed. "If he's still standing after he sees you, I'll be amazed."

~

Dan worked the room as the guests started to congregate. He'd done the basics having arrived thirty minutes earlier, ensuring he'd captured the venue and its dressings. While those weren't the images that would be readily used immediately afterwards, the seasoned pro knew they'd be used to promote the event in years to come.

Guests milled around, catching up with old friends and chatting to people they hadn't seen in a year and while Dan's camera was focused, his mind was elsewhere.

She'd be arriving soon. He had only seen her the day before, but he was nervous and excited to see her tonight, in equal measure. He couldn't wait to see her in the red dress she'd said she was buying for the event. Even though he was working, he'd made an effort with his outfit solely for her benefit. He knew he shouldn't. They were only friends but he wanted her to see him. Really see him. Like she hadn't before.

He started to edge across the ballroom, towards the foot of the large marble staircase, via which all the guests were slowly arriving. As grand entrances went it was right up there with the best and Dan figured that it would be a good place for him to be to ensure some nice arrival shots.

~

As they stepped through the top entrance to the Bailey Room, Sarah squeezed Laura's hand. "Go get him babe," then she descended the stairs ahead of her best friend. As she carefully walked down the marble staircase, (it wasn't easy being 6'1" in six inch heels) Sarah scanned the room for Dan. She eventually spotted him through the crowd in the ballroom below, taking photos of the guests. She knew she had to go and thank him in person for stepping in and helping out but now definitely wasn't the moment. There was someone else he needed to see first. Sarah smirked to herself. *You have no idea Dan. No idea at all.*

~

Dan looked up as if drawn by some force outside of himself and the world seemed to shift under his feet. There she stood at the top of the stairs, bathed in the light spilling from the nearby Christmas trees. She looked like an actual princess. His chest felt tight as he stared up at her. As she surveyed the ballroom below, you'd never have known she was once so nervous. Gone was the girl who stayed back in the shadows to appease everyone else, and in her place stood a radiant, self-assured woman, looking like a butterfly emerging from it's cocoon. To Dan, she was perfection personified.

Her black sequinned gown sat off her shoulders, highlighting a beautiful opal necklace, and slid down her curves, flowing out into a short train that now gathered around her feet. A long split ran up one side of the lower portion of the gown, and the soft skin of her leg could be seen from her ankle running all the way up to her mid thigh, with the briefest glimpse of a stocking top teasingly in view. The fabric of the gown seemed to shimmer in the lights of the ballroom, an array of colours twinkling in the light gently as she moved in matching dark heels.

She looks like an exquisite butterfly Dan thought to himself as he moved forward and she was taking flight in front of his eyes. In a dark corner of his heart, he knew he wouldn't ever be good enough for her.

He tried to breathe but the air felt like it had been sucked out of the room. He felt dizzy as he looked on and tried to make his way through the throng. There were so many people in his path. He knew, however, that only one person had to meet her at the bottom of the stairs and that person was him. She seemed to radiate class and pure sexiness as she made her way down the stairs, holding up part of her gown with one hand to help make her descent a little easier.

As Laura reached the bottom of the stairs, she found Dan waiting for her. No words were needed. She knew how good she looked. She knew he was staring because he couldn't speak. Twirling slowly and coming back to face the man who all of this was for, she simply asked, "will I do?"

Dan swallowed hard. And stared some more. He was lost in her. The world seemed to spin around her as she looked at him and smiled.

"Laura, you look beautiful. I…" he said, stammering a little. "You're exquisite." He wanted to tell her she was the most perfect woman to ever meet his eyes, he wanted to tell her that he'd never seen anything as beautiful as her in his life. But he steadied himself and instead held out his hand.

"May I have the honour of buying your first drink this evening?"

Laura blushed, but rather than taking his hand, slid her own hand up his forearm so she walked on his arm instead. "You may. And may I say you look very handsome. I don't think I could ever have imagined you in a suit, but you look very good in it." The thoughts in Laura's head were actually far less appropriate, so she kept those to herself.

As they walked the short distance to the bar, it felt like everyone was turning to watch them walk past. A year before, Laura would have hated that much attention on her. But now all she cared about was the man who walked beside her. It was his opinion that mattered and if his staring moments earlier was anything to go by, she'd achieved the effect she'd wanted for the evening. She felt peaceful.

~

A little while later, after finishing her meal, Laura made her way from the tables where the rest of the guests were enjoying their food, and headed to the bar to get a drink. She saw him sitting away to the side on his own. Once she'd paid for her glass of Prosecco, she made her way over to the quiet space he'd found for himself.

"Having a break?" She asked, making him jump.

His smile made her smile. "Yeah. No one likes photos taken mid-meal, so I'm having a few minutes. Plus my feet aren't used to dress shoes."

"May I?" Laura gestured to the empty stool next to him.

"You never have to ask to be in my company." Dan said, lost in her beauty, watching her sit.

He seemed sheepish as he sat looking at her. She knew she had him on the line, he'd taken the bait, but she wasn't quite ready to reel him in just yet. Not quite yet. The power she felt in the moment was intoxicating and she revelled in it.

"You seem quiet, Dan. Is something wrong?" Laura Gray had never been this coy and playful a damned day in her life but now she liked the game she was playing.

Dan smirked. Biting his lip. *Well, that's new* Laura thought to herself.

"It's hard, Laura, to be coherent around someone who looks this good in a dress like that. Even more so when it's you." He looked her up and down and finally settled on her eyes. And it made her growl inwardly. She wanted nothing more than to grab him and bite that pretty bottom lip of his and get completely lost in him. Laura knew he'd have no problem tearing her dress off right there and then, to claim what he wanted. But still, she kept him on her line.

For a second she glanced down at her right hand and her eyes lingered on the silver ring that sat on her finger. It must have been spun at least a thousand times through nerves and anxiety over the years. Realising that she wasn't nervous anymore, she carefully slipped it off and tucked it into her clutch bag, without Dan noticing. It made her feel a sense of freedom.

As they kept looking at each other, heat was building like a hot summer's night between them. It was getting dangerous. It would only take one of them to flinch and sparks would fly. But a large influx of guests approaching the bar cooled their fire and Laura left him to continue his evening's work.

"That suit really does look good on you." Now it was her turn to look him up and down, before rejoining her friends.

~

Dan needed a drink, but drinking on the job was something he never did. It was his rule and one he stuck to. He downed a fresh glass of iced water from the bar, tried to shake the fuzziness of Laura out of his head and got back to work.

~

Laura sipped her Prosecco and listened as the group of players she stood with discussed recent law changes in the game. Her mind was elsewhere but she needed to calm herself down. While it felt like there was a caged animal inside her, tense and waiting to break free and be primeval with Dan, another larger part of her was scared. Her body wanted one thing, her mind wanted another.

She didn't want to ruin their friendship by doing anything silly.

Yes she was in a good mood and enjoying teasing him but the idea of taking their friendship further that night terrified her. The scars Chris had marked her with were still deep and raw. She knew Dan was completely different, that he was incapable of hurting her but that didn't stop her fear around men. He had made her feel special and seen and she valued their friendship dearly. But playful flirting was one thing. Being wholly vulnerable in front of this man, ten years older than her, was something else entirely.

~

As he watched her laughing and smiling with the other guests, Dan slid behind one of the large leafy plants that decorated the outside edges of the ballroom. This allowed him to frame subjects in a different way through his lens and also to blend in with his surroundings a little.

She looked stunning.

He carefully worked through a short sequence of images as she smiled, waiting each time for her laugh or smile to be perfect before pressing the shutter. He was gentle and considerate, taking his time and working with purpose to capture Laura as he saw her, rather than as she often saw herself.

Minutes later he was walking away, focusing on other guests around the room. But he knew he had the perfect picture of her.

~

Was Dan just taking pictures of me? Laura could have sworn she'd sensed him nearby training his camera on her. But as she scanned the room around her she couldn't see him anywhere.

~

By 11pm, carriages were being called and the evening was at a close. Dan sat at a high bar table in the corner of the room in front of his laptop, importing the evening's images onto the small portable hard-drive he kept in his camera case. He was tired and his shirt collar was annoying him but it all faded away when he saw Laura floating towards him.

"Did you have a nice night?" He asked, still transfixed by how good she looked.

"It's been lovely. But it's time for Cinders to leave the ball now," she replied. She was tired but being with Dan made it worthwhile.

Standing from his stool, he hugged her. He felt her hands gently squeezing the muscles in his back as she melted into the embrace.

"You looked wonderful tonight," he whispered as her head rested on his shoulder.

Laura smiled. He always made her feel like she was the only person in the room no matter what room they were in.

"Message me when you get home so I know you're safe?" Dan asked. He worried about her when she wasn't with him.

Pulling herself gently from his arms she replied, "always."

Leaning in, she kissed his cheek and felt her face blushing. Biting her lip and dipping her head away from his gaze, she headed back to Sarah who waited for her at the bottom of the marble stairs they'd descended hours before.

The butterfly had her wings. Laura smiled. She finally felt like she was enough.

There will come a time in your life in which you will have to accept that your old ways cannot carry you any longer. You will know that it is time to light fire to the past and shed your old self. When the heaviness slows you to a stop, a reinvention must occur.

There will come a time in your life when you will realise that a new version of yourself is trying to emerge. You are allowed to cry and grieve the loss, but you must always keep your eyes toward what's next. It's time to wipe the slate clean and start again. It's time to break the chains of routine and expectation and fear. It's time to become different and stronger and clearer, at once new and yet more yourself than ever before.

~ *Brianna Wiest*

Chapter 30

Doin' everything I know to do, to keep the truth, from runnin' through my mind

Sarah slipped off her heels and kicked them into the footwell of the Uber. She was definitely on the side of tipsy but not so drunk that she couldn't make sense of things. It had been an enjoyable evening, getting to glam up, drink a lot of alcohol and catch up with friends away from the rugby pitch.

Beside her, sat her best friend, even though she was unrecognisable as the girl twelve months prior.

"Seems like you had a good night." Sarah said as she rubbed her sore feet; rugby boots she could do, heels less so.

"Ah Sarah, it's been lovely." Laura was tired but feeling the sort of contentment that touches your core. "I felt like an actual princess stood at the top of the stairs as he looked up at me. I melted."

"I don't think I've ever actually known Dan to be lost for words before, but I tell you what?" She said turning her head to her best friend.

"What?" Laura asked with a smile.

"That man knows how to wear a suit!"

"Yeah he does!" She replied. "That's a side of him I haven't seen before and it was…I'm not sure how to describe it?"

"Hot!" Sarah almost shouted, making the Uber driver flinch slightly in surprise.

Laura laughed. "Yeah, that pretty much covers it!"

He had looked amazing, she couldn't ignore that fact. She had always found him to be a good looking guy and the person he was, definitely was very attractive. Seeing Dan tonight in his classy black suit; from his crisp white shirt held together with a simple black tie, all the way down to his polished dress shoes, the man looked unbelievably handsome.

As she thought about it, Laura remembered how he'd looked at her as she joined him at the bottom of the stairs in the ballroom. Like no one else and nothing else mattered to him more than her. He had been an absolute gentleman the whole night, it had been nearly perfect. All that was missing had been the opportunity to dance with him. Laura had had this urge midway through the evening to spin around the dance floor with him, both of them getting lost in the music.

"Been a while since I've seen you this happy babe." Sarah commented.

Been a while since I felt this happy Laura mused.

~

The following morning Laura was nursing a hangover at the breakfast bar in her parents' kitchen, wondering if she should message Dan or not. She'd woken up feeling like she'd licked sandpaper and was very confused about the night before.

She felt like she was in a tug of war between her head and heart. Her heart wanted to run to him and not let him go, but her brain was telling her to hold back, worry and panic. Neither side was winning and it was only serving to make her head throb more.

Popping two paracetamol from the packet in front of her, she swallowed them with a mouthful of water and hoped they'd take the edge off.

Sitting in the kitchen, the morning winter sunshine, low in the sky, she understood why rock stars wore sunglasses indoors.

"You okay, Muffin?"

Laura warmed, hearing the pet name her dad always used when she wasn't feeling very well. The only thing was this sickness was self-inflicted and came with a Prosecco label on the packaging.

"Yeah just a bit worse for wear after a few too many last night," she replied, her mouth dry and her head sore. The world felt too bright this morning.

"Was it worth it?" Dave pulled up a stool at the breakfast bar next to his daughter, tea in hand and eyed the box of paracetamol that sat on the counter in front of her.

She smiled, "every moment Dad. I felt like a princess all night. It was really special."

"I'm glad. From the selfie you sent us, I can see why. You looked beautiful. We haven't seen that side of you for a long time, it was heartwarming to see after so long. Was Dan there?"

Knowing full well that her dad knew Dan was there, Laura raised an eyebrow. "You know he was, dad."

"Oh I was just wondering that's all," he replied coyly.

"He looked very lovely," she said, tailing off into her own thoughts.

"So why do you seem like you're stuck in your head this morning?" He asked, seeing right through her as usual, as though she was made of glass.

"I can't hide anything from you can I Dad?" Laura said, resting her throbbing head on her father's shoulder. "I like him. Dan I mean. And I didn't expect to. I don't know what to do."

Dave kissed the top of her head. He knew she was falling. He'd seen how she looked at Dan when they were together or how she smiled every time he messaged or called.

"Why are you worried?"

"What if he turns out like Chris? What if I'm not ready? What if I'm caught up in the attention and actually what I feel is temporary? I'm only just starting to feel like I can cope with life again but Dan is implicitly linked to that. What if I've made a horrible mistake and I can't stand on my own two feet?"

"Oh baby girl, you're a worrier, just like your mother." Dave smiled to himself. She was so much like Emily some days.

"Do you want my thoughts on it?" He asked.

"Please." She knew he was the only man she could ever truly trust and he always seemed to know what to say. *A bit like Dan in that regard,* she thought.

"I've only ever known one man to be as devoted to a woman as Dan is to you, Laura. That's how I am with your mother. You might be just friends at the moment, but I can tell you now as a man, he's only got eyes for you." Dave knew how Dan felt about his daughter, but he also knew it wasn't his place to reveal those feelings. That right belonged to Dan alone.

"You have to remember that you and Chris were so young

when you got together. You both went through a lot of changing and maturing in the time you were together. Unfortunately, it wasn't all for the better." Just saying Chris's name felt wrong, as Dave thought back to how her fiancé had changed for the worse over the years.

"But the thing about guys is, by the time they get to Dan's stage of life, they've done all the growing and changing they're going to do. He is the finished article now. He's figured himself out and he's got his shit together."

Laura thought back to sitting with Dan in Heathrow Airport and how he'd seemed like he was in control of his life.

"If you like Dan as more than a friend, then there's no rule book that says you have to get together now. You can wait and sit with the feelings you have, to see how you feel around him. If you two are meant to be together, if that's your fate, then time is irrelevant. If two hearts are meant to be together, no matter how long it takes, how far they go, and how tough it seems, fate will bring them together to share in their love forever."

"Dad, that's beautiful." Laura was on the verge of tears.

"Ah, your mum got me a quote a day book for my birthday," he joked, knowing that it would soften the moment for her slightly.

"Thought so," she chuckled into his shoulder. "Thanks, Dad. Thank you for always listening and being there for me."

"You don't have to thank me, Muffin. That's my job." He pulled her close.

"Dad?" Laura asked quietly. "How would you feel if Dan and I ended up being more than friends? Honestly?"

"I think it would make me and your mother very happy to

see someone love our daughter like she deserves. He's a good man."

"I'm scared."

Dave knew she was, but he also knew that somewhere past that fear lay everything she could ever want. "There's no guarantees in life, but I can promise you this - he couldn't ever be like Chris. He doesn't have that in him. You'll never have to live through that hurt again. He's brought you out the other side."

"Thanks again, Dad." Laura said feeling her hangover easing slightly. Hopping off her stool she kissed him on the cheek and went to get a shower, hoping it would wash away the after effects of the excess Prosecco from her body and mind.

~

Dave smiled and pulled out his phone.

Dave: Dan, what are your plans for Christmas Day?

He didn't judge me. He never picked me
apart to decipher my pros or cons. He simply
decided he wanted the whole package;
My insecurities along with my uniqueness.
And for the first time ever in a relationship,

CHAPTER 30

I saw myself blooming...
and I was stunning.

~Alfa

Chapter 31

"I'll buy you any star hanging in the sky"

Dave eyed Laura carefully. He could tell that even though it was Christmas Day, that she wasn't quite herself, as if she was hoping for something that she couldn't really articulate. He was silently willing her day to improve.

He'd given his little girl a huge bear hug earlier that morning and wished her a Merry Christmas when she'd woken up around 8am. She looked tired but at least she didn't look like she'd been crying all night. Dave was glad those nights were seemingly over as she had appeared to have turned a corner of late, since she had been spending more time with Dan. Even though she'd playfully pushed him away and started making a cup of tea, he still knew she wasn't feeling great.

~

Opening presents around the Christmas tree an hour later, Laura tried to be all smiles and happiness. She'd always loved gift giving even as a kid and being surprised by things she didn't expect. But this morning, as she watched her mother unwrapping a gift, Dave couldn't help noticing that she kept looking over at her phone every few minutes.

Another quiet but frustrated sigh moments later, prompted Dave to finally ask, "Muffin, what's wrong?"

Laura put her phone back down. "Nothing. I've just not heard from Dan yet and I kinda figured that on Christmas Day of all days, I would do. He's up. I know he is," she looked confused. "It's fine."

"Maybe he's just busy, honey," Laura's mother Emily suggested gently, as she carefully folded used wrapping paper.

"I guess." Something felt off and Laura couldn't put her finger on it.

Dave, sitting a few feet away from his daughter in his favourite armchair, knew it would be okay. "What did he get you anyway?"

Laura paused and didn't turn her gaze to her dad. "Nothing," she said quietly.

Dave was smiling on the inside. He knew what was coming and it would be better than any Christmas present she could imagine.

~

Later, Laura was in the kitchen helping her mother prepare

vegetables for dinner.

"Hey, go easy on those carrots! There will be nothing left at this rate."

Laura looked down at the massacred carrot on the chopping board and was saved from having to apologise, by her father calling her into the living room.

"Come here, Laura. I've got another present for you."

Confused, Laura put the knife down, to the relief of the other vegetables waiting to be chopped and went to see what her dad wanted.

"What..." She began to say as she walked into the front room and she stopped dead in her tracks.

"Merry Christmas."

Still in his big winter coat with a black scarf hanging from his neck, Dan stood with Dave in front of her, his blue eyes twinkling in the lights of the Christmas tree. He looked like a vision of festive loveliness.

Seeing him there set Laura free and she smiled, bursting into happy tears. Dave just grinned smugly and patted Dan on the shoulder.

"I'll go put the kettle on. Coffee Dan? Black, one sugar?"

"Please Dave. Thank you., Dan replied without ever taking his eyes from his favourite person, standing in front of him. He grinned broadly, it didn't just stop at his mouth. It seemed to extend through his whole face. A smile of complete happiness.

"I'm sorry I didn't message you this morning. It was your Dad's idea to keep you wondering."

"Oh, so this was all planned?" Laura said through her tears as she hugged him.

"You didn't think I wouldn't get you anything for Christmas did you? I knew this year would be your first on your own and even though you're here with your mum and dad, I knew it could be hard for you. So your dad and I spoke a few weeks ago and we agreed that I'd come over this morning to give you your present in person." He smiled as he hugged her.

"You two will be the death of me, I swear it!" Laura said as she removed herself from the hug so she could look up at her friend.

"Merry Christmas." Dan held out a present. It was beautifully wrapped in dark green paper. A red ribbon had been tied expertly around it and brought up into an elaborate bow in the centre. His handwriting was visible on a green tag that matched the paper, stuck to one corner of the gift.

To Laura. Merry Christmas. All my love. Dan x

"Dan you shouldn't have!" Laura exclaimed, "Oh my God I

daren't open it, it's too pretty!"

"Don't say that before you open it, it might be shit!" Dan joked.

Laura carefully unwrapped the present and discovered a fluffy pink scarf that felt warm and luxurious to the touch.

"It's for those cold mornings when you have to get up early for training," he explained.

"Oh Dan, it's beautiful. Thank you." She melted into another hug.

"You're welcome," he said, holding her to him for a heartbeat.

~

When her parents joined them with hot drinks, Laura sat in a state of blissful peace on the end of the big three seater sofa, watching her dad and Dan swapping stories. He looked like he belonged. She gently and almost subconsciously stroked the scarf that he'd given her and mewed quietly to herself.

Dan had been explaining that she had left her Christmas present at the studio for him earlier that week while he'd been away working. He took the time, in front of her parents, to thank her for the very thoughtful gift; a first edition of a book by his favourite author. Laura couldn't help but smile.

"So," Dan began, "I have a gift for both of you too." Laura looked on, confused as he produced a gift and handed it to her mother, Emily.

"Dan! You really shouldn't have!" Emily blushed as she took the present, looking at Laura who was sitting a few feet away, looking surprised.

The gift was delicately wrapped just as Laura's had been, but this was a flat rectangular shape and looked like a large book. *Maybe it's a photo book of his work?* Laura pondered. As Emily opened it, it was hard for Laura to see what it was but she heard her mother gasp in surprise.

"Dan, it's beautiful! When did you take this?" Emily asked.

Looking at Laura sat on the opposite side of the living room to him, Dan explained. "At the dinner dance the other week. She was talking with some friends. I was just in the right place at the right time."

"It's really lovely, thank you," Dave said, shaking Dan's hand.

"You're welcome. Merry Christmas," he sheepishly replied.

Emily smiled at her daughter and passed over the framed print Dan had given them. What met her eyes, was a black and white photo of her in all her finery at the ball. She couldn't work out where he'd hidden to take it but the image was a candid moment of her smiling and laughing with her friends. *When I felt him taking pictures of me!*

Laura remembered the girl looking back at her from the print, although she'd not seen her staring back from the mirror in so long. He truly had a gift. Dan had such a way of making her feel special.

She gently touched the frame where her own face looked back and she smiled. She finally felt like she was herself again. But this was a new normal. She felt as close to fixed as she could feel and in many ways, better and stronger than she had maybe ever been.

~

An hour later, after they'd all enjoyed coffee and bacon rolls, it was time for Dan to leave. Laura, still carrying her scarf in her hand, walked him to the front door.

"Do you have to go?" She asked, pouting a little.

"Enjoy Christmas dinner with your parents, you don't need me imposing. And anyway, my turkey dinner for one, won't eat itself." She knew he was trying to make light of it but she desperately wanted him to stay and never leave.

As she stood in front of him, he gently took the scarf from her hands and lovingly wrapped it around her neck, holding the ends in his hands and pulling her towards him ever so slightly.

"Not much would improve this Christmas to be honest. I'm very thankful for shitty coffee at 4am in Heathrow Airport and that's not something I ever thought I'd hear myself say," he leaned in as he spoke. She looked up and bit her lip slightly. "Thank you for making my Christmas morning special," he added.

"I should be the one saying that Dan," Laura said softly, leaning into him, "not sure I'll stop smiling all day."

Dan inched in slowly. "You never know, maybe this will be the first of many Christmas mornings we spend together."

"I like the idea of that tradition," Laura whispered breathlessly as she leaned in even closer. The scarf felt warm around her. He was so close. He smelt amazing, she couldn't drag her gaze away from his eyes and his lips. He looked so inviting.

Dan smiled and kissed her forehead. "Merry Christmas Laura," then withdrew and headed back to his car.

Laura sighed and smiled, contentedly as she leaned on the door frame and watched Dan walking back up the drive. She returned his wave as he climbed into the dark estate car, watched him pull away and then closed the door behind herself.

Her dad said something to her as she sat back down on the sofa, but she didn't hear anything, she was lost in her own little world looking down fondly at the scarf wrapped around her neck. She smiled and hugged it to her, in the same way he had held her close. It smelt like him. *Merry Christmas Dan,* she said to herself.

"Dan and Laura"

[Dan's voicemail]

Dan it's me! I'm in! Coach just rang. I got selected for the England squad! I'm going to the training camp! Dan I'm in! I can't believe it. Shit, I need to call my parents and tell them. Call me as soon as you get this!

Dan ended the voicemail message and put his phone face down on the desk. In front of him an email remained unanswered, agreeing to his quote for working with his biggest client yet. It should have been a triumphant moment for both of them but all he could think about was that she'd be gone for three weeks and he'd be gone for four days before that. Three and a half long, lonely weeks without her. His heart sank.

Chapter 32

"Being apart ain't easy on this love affair, two strangers learning to fall in love again."

Closing the door to her car, Laura sat behind the steering wheel and let the tears finally fall. She watched a plane take off in the distance and even though she knew Dan wasn't on it, her heart broke. Four days felt like it would be an eternity.

It wasn't that he would be gone for long, it was the fact that he'd be in different time zones and really busy, which would severely limit their time to talk for those agonisingly long four days. Sure she'd be busy training but the nights would be long and the days would feel empty without him around. She'd been so accustomed to seeing his face every day.

Her phone vibrated in her pocket.

Dan: Miss you already. x

A loud sob racked her body as she rested her head in her hands. She hadn't expected it to hurt like this. Dropping him at Departures & Check-in, she'd been sad, they both were.

He'd pull her into a hug, sensing that she was conflicted about him leaving.

"It'll work out fine. You and I have what it takes to make it," he'd said as he'd held her close.

"Alright smart guy," she'd replied, pulling herself out of the hug, playful hitting him in the chest and smiling. "Stop using song lyrics on me." *Who was she kidding, she loved it.* "I have something for you. For the plane." She added.

He looked back curiously, titling his head a little as he waited.

Laura pulled a book out of her bag. "I said the next time I saw you in an airport I'd lend you this." She smiled and a tear welled in her eye.

Dan smiled as she handed him *Colours,* the book he'd seen her with nearly a year ago in this very airport.

"I always keep my promises, Dan." She moved closer and rested her head on his shoulder, her hands sliding around him underneath his open jacket. He felt warm.

"Hey you," he said, stroking her hair gently, "I'll be back real soon. I promise."

"You're just saying that," she replied, not wanting to let him go.

"I always keep my promises, Laura," Dan kissed her temple, "I'll message you when I land."

As she watched him sliding up on the escalator to the security area moments later, it struck her like a wave. Four days. No smiles. No bright blues that she'd gotten so used to. No hearing his voice as they chatted over coffee. It hit home just how much he meant to her.

~

Now as she sat in her deathly silent car, with planes taking off and landing ahead of her, she just wanted to rush through the airport like some scene from a romantic movie, find him and kiss him. But she didn't. Instead she took a deep breath and turned the key in the car's ignition to pull out of the parking space.

When the engine started the radio came to life and a song she knew played, *"you found the light in me that I couldn't find, so when I'm all choked up but I can't find the words, every time we say goodbye, baby it hurts"*

Laura started to sing along but trailed off as she remembered the next line. "Are you fucking kidding me?" She said aloud and turned the radio off, instead preferring to listen to the sound of her car than the heartbreaking lyrics of GaGa.

~

As Dan zipped his camera case closed and wheeled it out of the security area, he unlocked his phone. The message read:

Laura: Miss you too. Going to Sarah's for lunch. Let me know when you board. X

He smiled like he always did when she messaged him, irrespective of the subject, but his heart still ached. Four days, in a different time zone while working nonstop was going to suck in the worst way.

He'd spoken to Sarah the day before, to ask that she'd keep an eye on her friend for him. He still worried about Laura, even now.

Sitting at the gate, taste-free airport coffee in hand, he thought back to when they had bumped into each other less than a year before. The pretty blonde girl, with the beautiful blue eyes had shaken his world like a bottle of pop and he'd been captivated every day since.

He smiled, as his head played through images and movies,moments of the last few months of his life with her. Watching her play rugby. Seeing her standing on his upper floor balcony wearing nothing but his favourite NFL jersey and a pair of fluffy socks. The way she'd taken his breath away at the ball, looking absolutely stunning. The laughs. The tears. Sharing spring rolls. All of it. This trip was going to be torture.

~

Laura rang the doorbell and waited.

"He's gone?" Sarah asked when she saw her best friend crying on the doorstep of her little flat.

Laura nodded and wiped her tears on her sleeve.

"Come here," Sarah said, pulling her distressed friend into a warm welcoming hug, closing the door behind them.

Laura just sobbed. Her heart, so unexpectedly broken, "I miss him already."

"I know you do babe," her friend said, stroking her blonde hair, "but he'll be back soon."

"I know, but..." Laura stammered, struggling to get the words out. "Why does it hurt so much, Sarah? It's four days for fuck sake! I don't understand it."

Sarah pulled back and smiled, cupping Laura's face with her hands. "Because, whether you want to admit it or not; Dan isn't a friend. You love him."

The truth hit her like a freight-train, slamming her into a reality she hadn't ever pictured herself in. But as Sarah spoke, Laura knew it was true, even though she'd never even really admitted it to herself. While Dan and Laura acted as friends do and for all intents and purposes they were the best of friends; they were inseparable and her heart was his.

She'd fallen hard. She could see it now. The words that hadn't found her lips yet were rooted deeply in her heart. He had brought her back from the brink of being lost.

She looked up at Sarah, tears in her eyes, "I love him."

"About time you admitted it to yourself!" Sarah chuckled.

"But he doesn't feel the same way. I know it." Laura replied.

Sarah leant in and looked her best friend in the eye. "Babe. He loves you too."

Laura was floored. She felt the world shift underneath her feet. She hoped and wanted to believe it was true. "What do you mean he loves me?"

"How have you *not* seen how devoted he is to you? He might not say it but he's in love with you; it's like watching a Hallmark movie," Sarah was watching the pieces fall into place. "You know, I love you doesn't always sound like I love you, right? Sometimes it sounds like - stay at mine tonight, I don't want you to be alone. Here's a scarf for when it's cold and you have early training. Let me know when you get home. Have you eaten today?"

She looked back, shocked as Sarah pointed out all the obvious signs she'd missed. All the care he took to make sure she was okay, the times he'd opened up and let her in when the rest of the world was shut out, how he always made her smile. "He loves me, Sarah. He actually loves me!"

Sarah just smiled and nodded.

"Fuck what do I do? I have to text him and tell him. He might not be in the air yet!"

"Whoa! Slow down!" Sarah steadied her best friend. "This is the sort of thing you need to talk about in person, not over text. He needs to see your face when you tell him how you feel so you can see how he feels too."

She nodded. Sarah was right. "Okay, I'll wait till he's back. Maybe I'll see if he wants to come over for dinner before we head off for camp."

I don't think most people understand what true love is. It's not the cheesy "couple goals" posts for Instagram. It's not the fancy dates, the happy hours, or the majestic nights laughing at silly movies. True love is waking up in the middle of the night to help you when you're sick because I don't want you to be sick alone. It's being your shoulder to cry on, to vent to. True love is being your biggest cheerleader and toughest critic. True love is looking at each other on a spiritual level, a level so deep, that you can feel them when they're gone. True love is six little words, "no matter what, I got you."

~Sylvester McNutt

Chapter 33

"But I've never been in love like this. It's out of my hands. I'm shameless"

His phone read 11:37pm, as Dan rolled onto his back. Lying on the three seater sofa at Laura's parents' place, he tried to find a comfortable position in which to sleep. It wasn't that the sofa was uncomfortable, but the whole environment felt foreign. Like when you stay in a random hotel room and are unable to settle because it all feels different. He'd been tossing and turning for the past half hour. It didn't help that jet-lag was still kicking his ass. Four days working in the heart of Toyko on very little sleep should have tired him out but skipping timezones quickly in just a matter of a few days had messed his body clock up.

~

Having spent the evening enjoying dinner and a few too many bottles of red wine with Laura and her parents to celebrate her getting into the England Squad and his return to the country, Emily had protested when Dan had suggested he'd get an Uber because he had drunk too much to drive himself home.

"I can make up the sofa. You're not getting an Uber!" Laura had just smiled when her parents had refused Dan's slightly tipsy suggestion that he'd get a taxi home. The evening had been hugely enjoyable and merry and she didn't want it to end. Emily's home cooked lasagne had been a real treat for Dan after a few days of eating out and hotel bar snacks and the evening had flown by, leaving all four of them a little inebriated. It felt good to be home.

Dan smiled as he thought back to how pretty Laura had looked all evening. She'd worn dark jeans and a plain pink t-shirt, leaving her hair down. He always liked it when she left her hair down. Simple, but she'd totally rocked it. It would be hard for anyone to take their eyes off her. Dan in particular was in awe of her.

~

"Do you play Dan?" Dave had asked, spotting the younger man spying the old nylon string guitar in the corner of the room. It was dusty and hadn't been played properly for quite a while, but Dave had always kept it in tune out of habit.

"Yeah he does but he doesn't play for people, right Dan?" Laura cut him off before he could get a word out, a twinkle in her eye daring him to defy her expectations.

"I...erm...yeah, play a bit." Dan looked at Laura, who had a mischievous *well you don't, do you?* look in her eyes.

One glass of wine into the evening and Dan's inhibitions were quickly getting stood down. *I'll show you* he thought playfully. Picking up the three quarter sized guitar, he knew just what to play as he'd been messing around with it for the past few weeks.

Laura cocked an eyebrow as he sat with the guitar on his lap and checked it was in tune as her parents waited expectantly. She doubted he'd actually go through with it. He'd been so defensive when she'd asked him about his guitar the first time she had been at his studio and he'd never made an effort to play around her.

Dan felt his nerves flare as he placed his fingers on the fretboard in the position for the first chord. He'd backed himself into a corner and had he not had a drink, he would never have taken things this far. He took a deep breath and began to play.

Within two bars Dave was smiling. He knew that song better than any other song he'd ever heard. He turned his head to see his daughter, lovingly transfixed as Dan played *Eyes of Blue,* her favourite song.

Goosebumps raised on her forearms as he worked through the first verse of her song, gently singing away. It wasn't just that he was laying himself bare in front of her parents and she understood how vulnerable he felt right now; it was that Dan had clearly taken the time to sit and learn her song. It spoke volumes.

After singing the chorus he came to a gentle stop. "That's all I know of it. It's not the best version, sorry I probably butchered it." Glass of wine or not, self-doubt was his ever-present companion.

"Nicely done. I guess Laura told you I used to play it to her as a baby," Dave said, as Dan rested the guitar up against the table. Laura noted that he was gentle with the things that mattered.

"She did," Dan smiled at her as he said it but noticed the

pleading look in her eyes, *don't mention the tattoo* it screamed.

"Yeah," Dave continued, "she's even got a tattoo of it, but she thinks we don't know about that." He winked at Dan.

Laura glared at her dad. "How?!"

"Honey, you're not that good at covering it up." Her mother laughed as she went to get more wine from the kitchen.

~

The conversation flowed easily all night. Dave had taken particular pleasure in embarrassing Laura to a delightful shade of red, retelling the story of when she was three and had tried to help him wash his car with a garden rake. Dan had laughed so hard he'd nearly fallen off his chair.

~

There had been a moment, between courses, when Laura's parents had gotten up to clear the plates and prepare the dessert. An easy playlist was streaming softly from the speaker on the sideboard on the far wall of the dining room. The air in the room felt heavy with the effects of decent wine, good food and even better company.

'Fall' by Kolby Cooper started to play and Laura stood up. Dan sipped his wine and his head felt fuzzy.

"Dance with me," Laura asked, standing next to him holding her hand out towards him expectantly.

"Ah Laura, I don't dance. I can't begin to describe how bad I am at it." He desperately needed an out. He couldn't be that close to her.

"Like you don't play guitar for people?" She asked. But how could he say no to those eyes and that smile?

Taking her hand he rose and let her pull him into her. She held him close and they started to move with the music. Dan held his breath and tried to remain calm. She smelled so good. The wine was making his head spin more than the dancing.

Laura hadn't really expected him to say yes but as they moved slowly around the room, her heart raced. He felt solid as he held her, like a tree that would never falter in a storm.

Forget about love and all its madness. The song played. And they kept dancing.

Dan looked down. He'd spent the first verse and part of the chorus avoiding making eye contact at all, but after a while it was too much to bear. Looking down he saw Laura looking up. Her eyes were like deep beautiful pools in which he wanted to drown.

All he wanted to do was tell her she was loved and that he'd fix her, even if it took everything from him. He'd die for her if that's what it took.

Forget about love and all this sadness, and fall with me. The song played. And they kept dancing.

"See?" Laura said softly, never breaking their gaze, "you can dance."

Dan smiled. She always managed to make him do that in spite of himself. "Clearly you're too drunk to tell that I'm treading on your toes."

Now it was Laura's turn to smile.

And they danced.

~

The magic was only broken when the song petered out slowly and for a heartbeat longer they looked at each other. Somehow it was as if the world had faded away with the music and it was just them. As it always felt it should be. Laura was starting to see that now. She was hopelessly and happily in love with him.

She could have sworn her mother was in the doorway watching out of the corner of her eye but by the time she turned to look, the woman was gone.

Laura looked into his eyes and melted. Dan looked down and she felt him tug gently at her back, drawing her to him. He wanted her and she wanted him just as much. His lips met hers and fireworks exploded in her brain, his mouth felt warm and delicious. He kissed her in the most perfect way possible. Laura felt heat. So much heat.

She took him by the hand and they left the dining room and climbed the stairs. They were in her bedroom, Dan pinning her up against the back of the closed door as his lips expertly kissed her exposed neck, dragging whimpers from her that she didn't know were there, just waiting to be released. Laura's hands were under Dan's all too familiar black T-shirt, as she dragged her nails softly across his hip bones just above the waistband of his blue jeans. She could feel a clock ticking away inside her. Tick. Tick. Tick.

They were on the bed. Somehow Laura was out of her clothes, laying naked and exposed as Dan worked kisses slowly and tantalisingly down her soft belly. Her back was arched. She wanted this. She needed this. Laura was biting her lip so hard she could taste blood in her mouth. She was his canvas and he knew the art he was creating with each protracted kiss, unlocking her with every brush of his hot lips against her cool skin.

Then she woke with a start, her heart racing in the night. The sheer shine of sweat hung on her flesh. *What the fuck was that?* She was wide awake. Looking at the clock on her nightstand, Laura saw it read 11:52pm. She must've only been asleep for a few minutes at best.

Laying back she tried to relax, but she was wide awake, her heart pounding like a jackhammer in her chest. She rolled onto her side; the side which would allow her to see Dan lying on the sofa beneath her, if she could see through solid floors. Her belly fizzed with a feeling she'd not felt in so long. *It was just a dream.*

She threw the covers off and crept out of bed.

~

A floor below, Dan smiled to himself as he relived the dance, and the way they returned to the table giggling as Dave and Emily came back in with dessert when the song had ended. With the effects of the wine wearing off, he laid back, staring up at the ceiling wishing he wasn't on the sofa but upstairs. His mind began to wander.

~

Having drifted off into a soft dream of kissing Laura in the rain, Dan was startled by the click of a closing door in the unfamiliar room. As he strained his eyes in the dark he saw a shape moving across the living room. It didn't seem like Dave, too small; and he couldn't comprehend why Emily would be here.

"Laura?"

She whispered quietly in the dark, "I can't sleep."

With no further words and without warning, she lifted the blanket laid loosely over Dan's bare chest and she slid onto the sofa next to him. His breath caught in his throat as her warm hand ran smoothly up over his stomach and came to rest high up on his chest.

"Are you ok?" Dan asked, his voice cracked, less from the

evening's wine and more from the fear flooding his mind.

"Mhmm. I'm right where I want to be. I needed you." And with that Laura's head came to rest next to her hand. "Is this okay?" She asked gently.

"Of course".

Dan tried to hold her close. He tried to keep his cool. He tried to feel like this wasn't a big deal. But the tension in his body wouldn't let him. In that moment, lying with the most beautiful woman in the world, holding her next to his skin, Dan was terrified and just wanted to cry.

He could feel her body pressed against his. She was warm. From the position she was in, Dan could make out she was probably still in the t-shirt she'd worn at dinner, but what else, if much at all, he couldn't tell. However, even with him still wearing his jeans, he could feel the heat from her thigh which she'd draped across his leg. She felt perfect. He had no other way to describe it. With other women he'd shared a bed with previously, it had always been uncomfortable somehow. Arms in the way. Hair itching his face. They were too hot. Somehow, it had always been unbearable in the end. But this was different. They seemed to fit together perfectly, like pieces of a cosmic puzzle.

Had Dan ceased to exist right there and then, he knew he'd leave this earth having experienced a personal sort of heaven. But the idea of this being a fleeting thing, was coursing terror through his veins. His hand, which he'd placed on top of

Laura's on his chest, trembled slightly.

"Are you cold? You're shaking." Laura didn't wait for him to answer, she just simply pulled the blanket further over them and snuggled in closer. Within a minute, she was breathing peacefully against his chest and Dan suspected she had fallen into an easy slumber. He kissed her forehead lightly and whispered. "Sleep well."

This was torture. Beautiful torture and Dan wanted it never to end. For a few minutes, he tried to take it in, absorb the feeling, in case he never felt this good ever again. The way she felt against his chest, enough weight so he knew she was there but not so much that it was uncomfortable. How warm she felt, like a bed feels on a chilly morning when you don't want to get out. The way she smelled, clean and fresh, like the cool air after a spring shower. How soft her hand felt in his, rested on his chest, like it had been made by God to fit in his perfectly. He took it all in.

He knew any guy in his position would most likely grasp this opportunity to take advantage of what was probably a half-naked girl in his arms. He could easily wake her and make a move. But Dan knew, even on a cellular level, that he could never improve on this moment. It was as perfect as it would ever be. So, even though he was terrified, he lay there with her, trying to simply be present in the moment and closed his eyes.

~

When he opened them again, it was morning and the sun was peeking through the cream curtains of Dave and Emily Gray's front room. He stretched automatically and realised that he was alone. Laura was gone and so was her warmth that until now, he hadn't known he badly needed. He could hear movement in the kitchen next door, so donning his t-shirt, made his way to find her and hopefully coffee.

"Morning mate. Sleep alright?"

Dan was surprised to instead see Dave, making a cup of tea on the far side of the kitchen.

"Erm yeah, not bad, thanks. Where's Laura?" He was still half asleep and confused. He felt like his brain needed to catch up.

"She's not up yet, mate. She won't be awake for a bit. Never is if she's not training early," he replied. "Coffee?"

So she left during the night? Or did I have too much wine? Dan was confused.

"Yeah, thanks Dave. I think I need one. Black, one sugar, please"

Otherworldly

They had a deep connection
a burning chemistry
they fit together
like they had always
known each other.
When she was around him
she felt more like herself.
There was a feeling
that this was bigger
than both of them.
She didn't understand it
but she knew it changed her
forever.
It was a different world now.

~N.R.Hart

Chapter 34

"All of the things that I want to say, just aren't coming out right."

"I can't take advantage of her mate. I just can't."

"Dan, it's not taking advantage of her if she's there pretty much telling you that she wants you."

Sitting in the local pub, over a lunchtime pint and an obscenely large mixed grill apiece, Martin was genuinely amazed at the self control his friend had shown when a gorgeous half-naked girl had been lying in his arms the night before. Sure, he knew Dan had been scared but to not even try to kiss the girl he was crazy about seemed like the sort of control that only Zen masters possessed.

"But until she says it in those words, in my mind I'll always be her friend. I can't go to her. She's got to come to me." Dan looked tired and confused.

"She has to cross the floor to you. I get it, dude but seriously, I'm in awe." There was no way Martin could get out of that sort of scenario without a cold shower.

"It's more than that, mate. It would break my heart more, for us to have one magical night and for that to be all that ever happened." His neck ached as he said it, the result of a bad night's sleep on the unfamiliar sofa and the tension of a frustrating situation. He rolled his head on his shoulders, attempting to relieve the tension. "I can't put my heart out there only for her not to feel the same. It would be too hard to have her right there and it all be taken away for me."

Martin looked at his friend and while he didn't understand the pain, he could feel it. "That hung up on her huh?"

Dan gave a forced half smile. "We're past hung up mate. She is a part of my soul I never knew was missing. I saw her two hours ago over breakfast and I already miss her like I've not seen her for months. Have you ever known me to be like this?"

His friend chuckled. "Nope. You're not usually this much of a miserable sod!"

They laughed.

"You need to tell her Dan, or it'll chew you up."

"She needs to cross the floor, Martin. She has to tell me she loves me first. Otherwise I'm terrified that I'll break this thing we have."

"When does she go away to camp?"

Dan sighed, "tomorrow."

~

Across town, Sarah sat on the old futon in her flat and watched Laura as she paced the floor.

"If he loves me then why didn't he take his chance last night? I know I'm not good at this stuff Sarah, but I thought guys would go for the T-shirt and underwear vibe."

Sarah smiled and shook her head. Her friend stopped her

pacing and looked at her. "What? What have I missed?"

"I love you but you're thinking with a small mindset. Dan isn't guys. Dan is *Dan,* a gentleman to the core. He isn't going to make a move on you just 'cos you're there flashing some leg and snuggling in close to him. In that situation he'll just want to hold you and keep you safe from whatever is keeping you awake."

"Then what the fuck do I do to show him? Because last night didn't work!" Laura wasn't annoyed, she was just out of ideas.

"He won't make the first move, babe. That's not the kind of guy he is. He's respectful. A guy our age, would take what you did last night, as a green light and you'd be telling him to chill this morning because he couldn't calm the fuck down. Dan's not like that. He's not looking for some quick fun under the covers. He wants to love you. It's a wildly different thing."

Laura sat on the futon next to her best friend and leaned back to look up at the ceiling. "You're right. I'm thinking he's a boy not a man. God I'm so inexperienced at this."

"Don't look at me for advice on this stuff," Sarah said with a smile. She'd been single forever, married to the sport she loved, "but you have to make the first move with Dan. And I don't mean jump his bones when you get the chance, although expect fireworks when that happens. You need to tell him how you feel, then he'll know you feel the same and *then* the sparks can fly. You're not inexperienced at this, you're just trying to run with Dan before you've shown him you can walk. You need to cross the floor to him so he knows you're ready."

In her heart, Laura knew it was true. She couldn't try to show

Dan how she felt, she just needed to be open with him and tell him. But it was scary. As she thought about it however, she realised that all her time with him had given her the confidence she needed to tell him anything. He had never judged her for anything, either verbally or in his expressions; the man didn't know how to judge her. The idea gave her hope.

"I'm going to ask him for coffee. Tomorrow. Before we leave for camp. I'll tell him then." She said, convincing herself more than Sarah.

when you spend your life feeling
misunderstood, out of place, as if
the frequency you send off isn't
picked up by anyone. the song of
your heart isn't heard by others
in the same way you hear it,
it can be lonely.

but then there comes a day when
someone picks up on your energy.
they hear your music, and for the
first time in your life you feel

heard. understood. seen. and that
connection is more powerful than
almost anything.

so if you find it or if you have
it – hold it close. because that's
a rare type of magic that should
never be wasted.

~topher kearby

Chapter 35

"Goodbye in her eyes."

Dan rolled over and checked the time on his phone. 8:23am. *Bollocks!* He groaned out loud. The heavy feeling of jet-lag still held him and he'd ended up being in bed longer than he wanted. Now if he didn't get his ass in gear, he'd be late.

Lying there, looking through the skylight above his head, he saw the gathering grey clouds and wondered if it was a sign. He'd just got back. He didn't want her to go now. Four days had been tough and he knew she'd struggled a lot, but two nights before they'd had a near perfect evening with her parents, so the idea of her leaving for three fucking weeks was unimaginable. He could still feel the weight of her head on his chest and wished she was in his bed right now.

Throwing the covers off, he grabbed his phone and headed to the shower.

Dan: Hey you! Just getting a shower and then I'll be leaving. Overslept a bit this morning. Sorry x

Stepping under the hot rain shower, Dan hoped it would wash

away his sleepiness as well his sadness at her leaving; torn by conflicting feelings of loss at her imminent departure and pride that she'd achieved her dream, the one that she'd worked so hard for these past few months.

~

Laura sat waiting in the Rainbow Room Cafe, absentmindedly stirring her coffee, trying to quell the rising nerves in her belly. Yes, she was going away for three weeks, but he had to know how she felt about him, she knew she had to tell him. Two nights previously, she'd hoped he'd have figured it out when she lay with him in the dark on her parents' sofa, but for some reason he'd frozen and she'd fallen asleep on him, completely at ease in his arms. *Stupid man.* She smiled to herself. He was far from stupid. He was smart, witty, wildly practical and emotionally intelligent. Anything but stupid.

As she waited, she mused on her location at the back of the cafe. She'd wanted to pick somewhere quiet and hidden away. Looking around, she realised she had the right table. While she was nervous, she was also in a playful mood this morning, wanting to see how quickly he would find her. Like a grown up game of hide and seek, where the prize was mediocre coffee and her company. She smiled to herself at her brilliance. *I've been smiling a lot recently.*

She knew in her heart that she loved him, but the question of his love for her in return, remained as yet unanswered. Laura of a year ago, would never even contemplate the idea of telling him she loved him. The fear of rejection would have been too massive to deal with.

But she was stronger now. He'd become the glue that held her together. She knew that for sure. But it was more than that. He was like the golden joinery that the Japanese used to repair broken pottery. It made everything more beautiful than the original. Dan did that. He'd fixed her pieces and made her more beautiful in the process, like the princess that had attended the ball weeks earlier. She felt like she could tell him anything; even that she loved him and it would be okay.

~

The cafe door chimed as he entered. Her inner animal purred as she watched him unzip his big winter jacket to reveal his signature black t-shirt and blue jeans underneath. He looked really cute this morning, his hair still a little fluffy and damp from his morning shower. His short trimmed beard and his bright blue eyes seemed to stir a fire in her that she didn't care to extinguish any more, preferring to just let it burn. She bit her lip but reminded herself to chill the fuck out. He searched the small cafe to find her and his eyes settled on her, sitting in the back of the room. The purring was now a full on growl. *Down girl* she told herself.

He made his way to the counter and ordered himself a coffee. She didn't need to see what he'd ordered to know exactly what he'd have. Black coffee, one sugar. Always. It was one of the constants about him that she found comforting. Dan had these little habits that made her feel at peace. The coffee he drank. The colour of t-shirts he wore. How he would always hold doors for her. The little things that made her feel like everything would be okay.

But comfort or not, her nerves seemed to be simmering close to the boil. She was literally planning to put her life and her heart in his hands.

"Morning! I swear this coffee smells good today. Either that or my ability to appreciate good coffee is waning over time. Is that a sign of old age, do you think? A diminished sense of smell and the lack of appreciation for fine things?" Dan smiled at her as he pulled out the chair opposite and sat down, placing his coffee in front of him.

"You know full well that the coffee is as bad as it was the first time we came here and it isn't getting any better anytime soon."

That made him chuckle. She liked having that effect on him.

Dan looked at Laura and smiled. "Sleep well?"

"Pretty good. I'll probably sleep in the hotel later for a little bit."

For a moment there was silence. Both of them realising what that meant today and not wanting to vocalise it or deal with it, they just let it hang in the air for a heartbeat.

"Don't worry, I'll come up to camp in a few days and sneak in to see you." He could see her unease creeping in.

"I might just tell them to not let you in." She joked and winked at him.

Their eyes met and Dan smirked back, that half smile he did, always trying to be cool. She liked having that effect on him too. He had a really pretty smile. She made no effort to stop herself swooning, *what was the point any more*?

"We'll see."

~

The pair sat chatting and joking with each other as life in the coffee shop evolved around them. They were lost in their own little universe as the outside world passed by. It had been this way for what felt like the last six months, just the two of them together as the world fizzed around them.

The hour they had to share coffee and company before she needed to leave for camp passed too quickly and before long it was time to leave.

"Fancy walking me back to Mum and Dad's? You can do the big emotional goodbye waving me off in my car if you like." Laura desperately hoped the plan she was about to put into action would work.

Dan showily checked his watch and mocked, "ah I dunno, I'm kinda busy this morning." Seeing her pout, added, "But I can spare a little bit of time for you."

~

As they left the cafe, they walked in silence. Both of them lost in their own awkward thoughts. Dan didn't want her to go, he'd been without her for the past few days; the idea of three more weeks without seeing her seemed insurmountable. Walking next to him, Laura's stomach was in knots as she went over the plan in her head anxiously holding on to the hope that he loved her back.

Arriving at the top of the drive at her parents' house, he stood awkwardly in front of her. He looked distracted and uncomfortable, but she just put it down to the fact he was gonna miss her. And maybe a little bit of lingering jet-lag.

"Hey, it's okay," she said as she pulled him into a hug. They'd hugged countless times before but this felt different. This felt somewhat final and Laura didn't like it.

"I'm going to miss you," she whispered. Laura felt Dan slump into her embrace.

"I'm going to miss you too. I hate this. I've only just got back. You'll call me when you get there?" He asked in a whisper.

Pulling her face from his chest, she nodded. *Damn he smelled good,* Laura placed her hands at his side, tugging gently on his jacket and looked up at him. He was struggling with something, Laura knew it but she couldn't worry about that now. She had to let him know. Still part of her was afraid of getting this wrong, afraid of having read the signs wrong and of making a huge fool of herself.

"Hey" she lifted his chin and looked into his piercing blue eyes. Dan looked away and didn't meet her gaze.

"Hey, it's okay," Laura repeated softly.

The man, who she'd fallen for, looked down. She felt it. That spark. The need to just be with him here and now and forget everything else. It was now or never. This was it.

Laura moved closer to Dan who kept his eyes fixed on her face as if trying to commit it to memory. Their foreheads met and for the briefest of moments they breathed together in unison, and nothing else existed, their worlds as one. It was just them in the moment.

It's now or never, Laura told herself as she leant up to kiss him. Dan hesitated. Undeterred, Laura moved in again and their lips met for the first time. But something was off. This was a one sided kiss and she was the only one in it. Confused, she pulled back and looked away.

"Laura, we shouldn't. I'm sorry," Dan said, as they stood there awkwardly.

"It's fine. Whatever. See you when I'm back," Laura muttered as she hurried down the drive. She could feel the confusion and hurt building inside her. *WTF was that?*

Chapter 36

"baby, the truth is you're all that I need."

"Laura, wait!" Uncharacteristically, Dan shouted her name.

She didn't look back and rushed towards the house. "It's fine Dan, just forget it!" She called over her shoulder. She was six feet from the front door when he spoke quietly.

"Laura, the reason I didn't kiss you back is that I was afraid. Afraid that if I did, I'd never want to stop kissing you." He paused. "I love you. I've always loved you."

Laura stopped but kept her eyes on the door in front of her. She didn't know what she was waiting for but something prevented her from going into the house and even though she didn't turn around, her heart hurt. She felt raw, like an opened wound.

Hearing the commotion, her mother rushed to the front door

to see what was going on. She'd never heard Dan raise his voice and this was so out of character for him, she assumed something was wrong.

Emily held her breath, desperate to shout to her husband who was watching the news in the living room. Her eyes turned first to her daughter and then to Dan. Without a glance back, Laura walked past her car, down the last part of the driveway, past her waiting mother in the doorway and slumped on the bottom step of the stairs in the hallway, staring down at her hands. They were shaking. *Where's my fucking ring?!* Time seemed to stop. The only noise she could hear was the pounding of her heart in her ears.

He loves me, yeah? Laura thought. *So why didn't he kiss me back?*

Tears welled in her eyes as she sat there wringing her hands in the deafening silence all around her as she thought about everything he had become to her. She heard the front door shut and her mother quietly breathing next to her.

"Erm, what just happened?" Emily said, looking at her daughter.

"Dan just told me he loved me." Laura replied without any pause or emotion. Dave, now in the doorway to the family living room, stood open-mouthed, his mug of tea still clasped in his hand. He knew that Dan loved his daughter without condition or agenda but he hadn't expected this!

Laura was desperately trying to hold back the floodgates she knew could burst at any moment.

"So let me get this right? A guy that you've not stopped talking about for months, who you are clearly crazy about, just declared his love for you openly like a scene from a movie in what is probably the most romantic gesture I've ever seen?" Her mother asked.

"Yup."

"And you're sitting here, why?"

Laura paused. The numbness in her bottom lip, told her she'd been chewing on it since she'd sat down. Her heart was still hammering away in her chest as she frantically tried to find a reasonable explanation as to why she was still sitting staring at her hands.

"Laura!" Her dad said aghast, from the living room door to her right, 'if you don't go after him and kiss him, I will! And he's not even my type!"

Like a vice on her heart, fear of losing Dan forever gripped her tight. She looked at her parents who stared back in shock. Steeling herself, she bolted out of the front door and rushed up the driveway, finding him sitting on the kerb a few houses along.

~

"What do you mean you love me?"

Dan stared at the tarmac in front of him, tearing apart a blade of grass he'd pulled from a crack in the pavement.

The secret was out now. There was no way to put it back in its tidy little box and deny everything. His heart ached and he knew he'd probably ruined everything, losing a beautiful friend in the process.

He'd always promised himself that he'd let her say it first, before he ever told her how he felt. But feeling Laura kiss him, those soft warm lips against his, he had panicked. Seeing her rush away from him, fearing he'd lose her forever, the burden of hiding his true feelings from her became too much to bear.

He kept staring at the ground, scared to look at her. Afraid that the way she looked at him would now be changed forever.

Laura was still reeling. "Dan, please!" She begged. She couldn't move. The adrenaline mixed with fear that had forced her through her parents' front door had now vanished and she found herself unable to move, ten feet from Dan, still sitting on the kerb.

Dan let out a long sigh. "I'm in love with you, Laura. I'm in love with everything you were, everything you are and everything you will be, yet to come. You're the piece of me I've been searching for my whole life. The part of me I never knew was missing."

"Dan..." Laura was out of words. Her head hurt and the world was spinning out of control.

The secret was out, he reminded himself. He thought about the tattoo on his forearm. *Go big or go home.*

Keeping his eyes fixed on the blade of grass and the tarmac in front of him, he continued. "You remember that photo shoot a couple years back? The one we did with Sarah? There was a moment early on, during the first set up, that I got an image of you. It was never used in the campaign but the moment I saw it on the back of my camera, I was drawn to you. I've looked at that image a thousand times since Laura; I can't tell you what it was that drew me in because I don't know. But for the rest of the day I couldn't take my eyes off you. I've been in love with you ever since.

Have you ever wondered why I couldn't talk to you properly the first few times we saw each other? It wasn't nervousness so much, more that I couldn't breathe around you. I've never been able to fully gather my thoughts around you. That's the effect you have on me.

In the early days it was easy. We never saw each other and I knew you were engaged. So it was easy to stay away and bury my feelings. I tried to get you out of my head. I didn't want to be the guy who tried to break up a relationship. From what I knew, you were happy. I didn't want to steal that from you.

When I heard about you and Chris, I was devastated for you. I knew how much that would have hurt. Then seeing you again in Heathrow last year, it just brought all those feelings I thought I'd buried for so long, back to the surface.

I've only ever wanted you to be happy, Laura. For the past few months, I saw our friendship doing that. That's why I've never said anything. It was never a long play to find my way to your heart or anything like that. You needed a friend and I wanted to be around you, to see you happy. That's it. That's all I've ever wanted. If nothing happens from now and we just stay friends, I'm absolutely okay with that, you have to understand. I know I've probably just fucked this up.

You deserve the best life with a guy who can make you happy and give you everything you want. I know that's probably not me. I get it. But I will give you whatever you need to help you achieve that."

Laura thought about how wrong he'd got it. He still thought she wanted to be his friend. He hadn't realised that she was lost in him and never wanted to be found again.

With tears welling in his eyes, Dan finally stood and faced the woman he loved with every fibre of his being. He tried to smile through the pain.

"I've loved you for so long, Laura. And I will keep on loving you until I'm dust in the ground. But you don't have to love me back. I'm happy just to be around you and see you smile."

Laura had given up trying to hold the tears back and they now poured freely down her soft cheeks and on to her training top.

"You're such a fool." She whispered through now happy tears. Dan looked confused.

Closing the distance between them in a heartbeat, she threw her arms around Dan's neck and kissed him as if he'd been lost to her for a lifetime. And this time, Dan kissed her back. His hand came up and gently cupped her beautiful face as they melted into each other, in the kind of kiss that freezes time.

Parting finally, they looked at each other and laughed. Dan brushed Laura's cheek with the pad of his thumb as she looked deeply into his eyes.

"I love you too," she whispered through her tears, as he felt the missing piece click into place.

CHAPTER 36

Dedicated to all the Lauras who were loved but never knew

Epilogue

Laura rested her head on Dan's chest and sighed a long contented sigh, his right hand drawing gentle circles on the small of her back. Kissing his chest, she moaned slightly.

"Mmm stop it or we'll never make it out of this bed alive," she purred. Draping her leg over his bare thigh, they lay there in the afternoon light in a naked tangled mess of post orgasmic bliss.

Returning from Camp three days earlier, sore and tired but hugely content, Laura had spent most of her time at Dan's studio apartment. When they weren't making love, they were eating, sleeping and drinking coffee together, not wasting any time apart. She'd even put her phone charger on the empty side of the bed; like putting a flag in the ground, claiming that side of the bed in the name of Laura Gray.

That afternoon, after brunch with her parents, she'd headed back to Dan's where he'd whisked her off to bed the moment she'd arrived and made love to her for hours until the early evening light scattered through his studio. She'd never experienced anything like it. She wasn't just his sole focus in life but always his entire focus in the bedroom. It left her feeling deliciously spoilt.

Rolling onto her back and dragging the covers over her bare

stomach to retain some level of warmth, she smiled. The motion seemed to bring Dan even closer and with a slight movement down the bed he placed kisses on her belly moving slowly higher, until he was kissing her collarbones.

"God, Dan stop! We should be getting dressed and going for dinner. Remember dinner? With my parents at six?" It might have sounded like a protest but she didn't move at all, aside from bringing her hand up to play with his hair, closing her eyes as he worked his lips up her naked body.

"Nope. Don't remember dinner. Sorry. I guess I should stay here doing this indefinitely," he said in between soft, delicate kisses.

Laura chuckled. "Dan, you know I want to stay here indefinitely but we have a dinner to get to. And as it stands I'm not even sure if my legs actually work anymore!"

"Then stay here forever. You claimed ownership of this bed once before, it's yours. Like I am," he breathed between kisses.

Fucking hell what's he doing to me Laura thought as the passion in her flared again.

"Dan, I want to be with you forever." As she said it she realised there was less passion and more truth in her words. She really didn't want to ever be apart from him.

His kisses stopped and he looked up at her, resting his chin on her chest with a serious expression on his face. "Do you mean that?"

She knew what he was insinuating. "Yeah. I know it's only been a few weeks but you're my happily ever after Dan." Gently stroking the side of his face she added, "I know it in my bones."

Dan smiled and rolled away, reaching into a small drawer located under his nightstand, which was home to his framed picture of his parents and his dad's wedding ring. He turned back to her holding something in his hand.

"So, while you were in camp, I went to visit the storage unit where a lot of my parents' stuff has been kept since they passed away. It's mostly furniture and paintings and stuff but there's a few little bits I kept. Do you remember what I told you about them?"

Laura snuggled into him closer. "Yeah. That they were your model for what true love is; you told me they were the greatest love story ever told. Which may I add, is the most adorable thing you've ever said!"

"Yeah they were. While you were away, I went to collect something I left there. When you told me you loved me before you left for camp, I knew that one day it would be time to write a new love story, like theirs."

He rested a small box on her chest. .

"This belonged to my mother," he said, opening the box and looking at her.

"Dan. What are you saying?"

Inside the box, was a beautiful diamond ring that seemed to shimmer in the light of the bedroom. The stunning diamond sat on a simple silver band. It looked incredible.

"I'm saying that I love you Laura and I always have. I want to spend my future with you making memories that are just for us, if you'll have me. I want us to tell a new love story like my parents did, one that's about us."

Laura's eyes were welling up so much it made the diamond ring seem to sparkle even more.

"I've already spoken to your parents, and even though I said

I probably wouldn't do this for a very long time to come, I did ask them if they'd be okay with me marrying you one day."

She held her hand to her mouth, partly in shock and partly to stop the excitement escaping her mouth. He gently took the ring out of the box and carefully held it in his fingers. Looking her in the eyes and smiling that half smile of his that she'd fallen so much in love with, he asked.

"Laura, will you marry me?"

"Yes! A thousand times yes!" She said as he tenderly placed the ring on her finger. They were both crying as she kissed him and wrapped her arms around him.

"I'm in this for life, baby," he said as she took a moment to look at the ring on her finger.

"Me too!" She said, and she meant it. Everything was finally right with the world.

I am not the first person you loved.
You are not the first person I looked at
with a mouthful of forevers. We
have both known loss like the sharp edge
of a knife. We have both lived with lips
more scar tissue than skin. Our love came
unannounced in the middle of the night.
Our love came when we'd given up
on asking love to come. I think
that has to be part

of its miracle.
This is how we heal.
I will kiss you like forgiveness. You
will hold me like I'm hope. Our arms
will bandage and we will press promises
between us like flowers in a book.
I will write sonnets to the salt of sweat
on your skin. I will write novels to the scar
on your nose. I will write a dictionary
of all the words I have used trying
to describe the way it feels to have finally,
finally found you.
And I will not be afraid
of your scars.
I know sometimes
it's still hard to let me see you
in all your cracked perfection,
but please know:
whether it's the days you burn
more brilliant than the sun
or the nights you collapse into my lap
your body broken into a thousand questions,
you are the most beautiful thing I've ever seen.
I will love you when you are a still day.
I will love you when you are a hurricane.

~Clementine von Radics,

About the Author

Eliza Hope Brown, born in rural Wiltshire, is a full time writer of contemporary fiction. She studied English and Foreign Languages at DeMonfort University and was a primary teacher and graphic designer before writing her first novel in late 2022. She lives in London with her cat, Morley.

Also by Eliza Hope-Brown

Coming soon: *Colours* (expected 2023)

Sweet Inevitably Series

Different universes. Different timelines. Different iterations of the same people.

Can Dan and Laura find their matching pieces in every world?

The same hearts, different lives. Will love find a way?

This time around Laura and Dan have been friends for a lifetime.

Their families have been close friends forever.

One of them falls in love with someone unexpected, one of them takes up a dream job on another continent.

If you liked *Sanctuary,* you'll love *Colours.* The second installment of the *Sweet Inevitability* series